some self-defense," Mark announced.
"Put your arms around me."

As Vanessa followed Mark's order, forbidden excitement shot thought her.

"There are several ways to respond to an attack. Stomp your attacker's foot. Scrape his shin with your heel. Or bend your knee for a backward kick to the groin. Got that?"

"Yes." She's also gotten hot and bothered by their close contact. Her cheeks were flushed, and her forehead was damp with sweat. A princess was not allowed to sweat.

He made her feel alive. A sexy and intense chemistry sizzled between them.

"Good."

"Mmm, good." She had no idea what he was talking about. She felt dreamy and distracted.

"But sometimes—" He snared her in his arms, flashed a devilishly sexy smile and lowered his head until his lips almost brushed hers. "Sometimes your attacker might use a devious approach. Will you be prepared for this?"

Before she could think, his mouth captured hers.

Dear Reader,

Celebrate the holidays with Silhouette Romance! We strive to deliver emotional, fast-paced stories that suit your every mood—each and every month. Why not give the gift of love this year by sending your best friends and family members one of our heartwarming books?

Sandra Paul's *The Makeover Takeover* is the latest page-turner in the popular HAVING THE BOSS'S BABY series. In Teresa Southwick's *If You Don't Know by Now,* the third in the DESTINY, TEXAS series, Maggie Benson is shocked when Jack Riley comes back into her life—and their child's!

I'm also excited to announce that this month marks the return of two cherished authors to Silhouette Romance. Gifted at weaving intensely dramatic stories, Laurey Bright once again thrills Romance readers with her VIRGIN BRIDES title, *Marrying Marcus.* Judith McWilliams's charming tale, *The Summer Proposal,* will delight her throngs of devoted fans and have us all yearning for more!

As a special treat, we have two fresh and original royalty-themed stories. In *The Marine & the Princess,* Cathie Linz pits a hardened military man against an impetuous princess. Nicole Burnham's *Going to the Castle* tells of a duty-bound prince who escapes his castle walls and ends up with a beautiful refugee-camp worker.

We promise to deliver more exciting new titles in the coming year. Make it your New Year's resolution to read them all!

Happy reading!

Mary-Theresa Hussey

Mary-Theresa Hussey
Senior Editor

Please address questions and book requests to:
Silhouette Reader Service
U.S.: 3010 Walden Ave., P.O. Box 1325, Buffalo, NY 14269
Canadian: P.O. Box 609, Fort Erie, Ont. L2A 5X3

The Marine &
the Princess

CATHIE LINZ

SILHOUETTE *Romance*®

Published by Silhouette Books

America's Publisher of Contemporary Romance

For Alison Hart, aka Jennifer Greene,
for being such a wonderful friend over the years
and for sharing my love of fairy tales. And with
very special thanks to my editor, Jennifer Walsh,
for making the entire process such a creative pleasure.

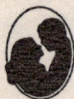

SILHOUETTE BOOKS

RECYCLED PAPER

ISBN 0-373-19561-3

THE MARINE & THE PRINCESS

CATHIE LINZ

left her career in a university law library to become a *USA Today* bestselling author of contemporary romances. She is the recipient of the highly coveted Storyteller of the Year Award given by *Romantic Times Magazine* and was recently nominated for a Love and Laughter Career Achievement Award for the delightful humor in her books.

Cathie enjoys traveling, spending time with her family, her two cats, her trusty word processor and her hidden cache of Oreo cookies!

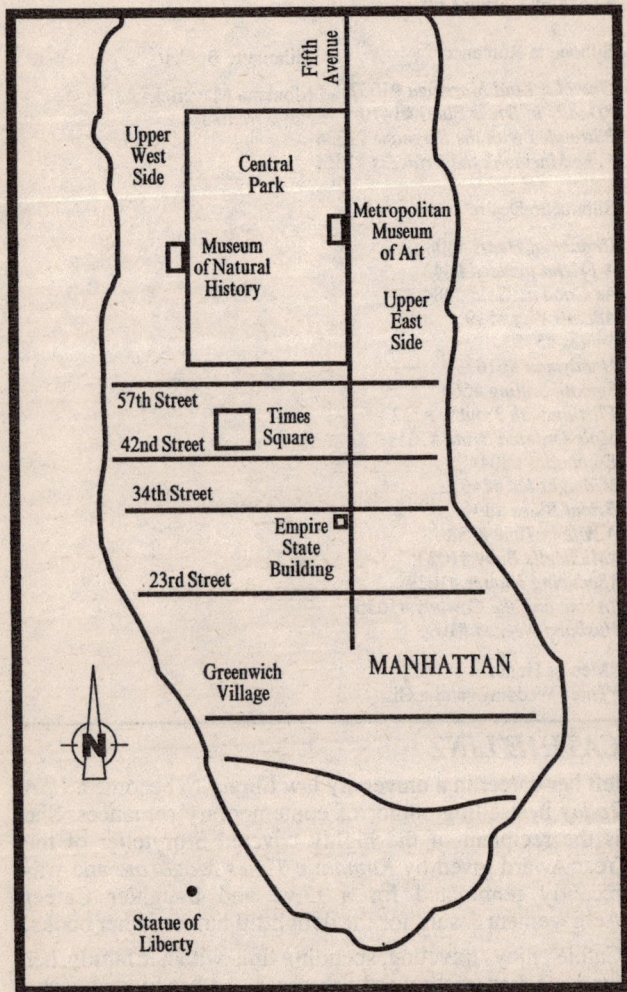

Fifth Avenue

Upper West Side

Central Park

Museum of Natural History

Metropolitan Museum of Art

Upper East Side

57th Street

42nd Street

Times Square

34th Street

Empire State Building

23rd Street

Greenwich Village

MANHATTAN

N

Statue of Liberty

Chapter One

"**Y**ou've got to help me!" Princess Vanessa Alexandria Maria Teresa Von Volzemburg pleaded in desperation.

"What's wrong?" her close friend Prudence Martin-Wilder asked from the other end of the phone line. "Are you okay?"

"No, I'm not okay," Vanessa replied, kicking off her designer shoes and flinging herself onto the ivory damask-covered chaise lounge in her suite at the Plaza Hotel. "If I have to shake another hand or smile another empty royal smile I'm going to scream." Her voice was shaky with exhaustion. "Here I am in New York City, the most vibrant and exciting city in the world, and I'm locked up like a prisoner."

Vanessa stared out the hotel window at the sparkling city lights with longing. A big world was teeming with life out there. Without her.

She felt so trapped. Her prison walls were invisible bars constructed out of ingrained loyalty to her family and her country. She was burned-out from months and months of continuous projects—racing from one official function to another, putting duty above her own health, working through two bouts of flu and one of bronchitis, not pausing for illness or fatigue until she was so depleted she couldn't even think straight anymore.

"What are you doing in New York?" Prudence asked.

Vanessa rubbed her sore feet. You'd think shoes that cost several thousand dollars and had been made just for her would be comfortable as well as stunning. Many was the time she'd longed to show up for some formal occasion wearing an old pair of broken-in athletic shoes under her Valentino haute couture gown. "I'm here for the International Chocolate Manufacturers Convention promoting the chocolate makers of Volzemburg."

"A tough job, I know, but someone has to do it," Prudence said in a teasing voice.

"I've been working since six this morning, and it's now after eleven at night. It's been like that every day. I don't think I'll be able to look at another chocolate truffle for a month," Vanessa groaned.

Prudence laughed. "I find that hard to believe."

"Okay, so maybe I'll be ready for more chocolate in an hour or two. But I *won't* be ready to return to Volzemburg." Vanessa shoved restless trembling fingers through her shoulder-length blond hair, ruining the smooth line of her expensive cut. The royal hairdresser Mimi would be distraught at the way Vanessa's hair looked now. Tough noogies. "My father has been driving me crazy with his demands that I announce my engagement to Sebastian de Koonan."

"Sebastian...he's that wealthy business tycoon from Volzemburg, right?" Prudence asked.

"Right. His lineage is almost as good as mine. And he's good-looking in his own way, I suppose. But the idea of marrying him…" Vanessa shuddered. "It would be like marrying my brother or cousin. I just don't feel that way about him."

"Have you told your father that?"

"Yes, certainly I've told him, but my father doesn't listen to me. I can't take this anymore!" Her voice cracked. "I've got to get out of this prison of responsibilities, even if only for a few days."

"Now, Vanessa, don't do anything rash," Prudence warned, clearly recognizing that tone of voice from their teenage days when they'd both attended a private girls' school together for a year.

"Don't do anything rash?" Vanessa repeated. "This from a woman who went bungee jumping?"

"Yes, well, I'm not a princess. As you said at the time, you do have responsibilities. You can't just take off on a vacation or something."

"I can't?" Vanessa sat up a little straighter. "Why not?"

"Because your life is planned out months in advance, your royal schedule booked down to the last second. Isn't that what you told me?"

"Yes, but next week my father has me spending time with Sebastian at the palace. There aren't any major charity functions or official business events planned." Excitement took hold and for the first time Vanessa began to see a glimmer of light at the end of what had been a very long, dark and lonely tunnel for her. "I could just take off."

"No, you couldn't. That would be dangerous. You're a wealthy princess. If you went missing your father would send out the Marines for you, or the Volzemburg equivalent of that." Prudence's father was a sergeant major in the U.S. Marine Corps, and last year she'd married a Marine, so she tended to voice things in Marine-like terms.

"Ah, but I wouldn't go missing," Vanessa said. "I could stay right here in New York City."

"Your father wouldn't let you do that."

"He would if he thought I was sick. And I have been sick. I'm so beat that I'm sure I'm about to come down with something. Yes." Vanessa cast a determined look around the well-appointed room. "I need a rest from this prison. And I have a plan that I think will work!"

"I think it's crazy."

"You haven't even heard it yet," Vanessa protested.

Prudence sighed. "Okay, go ahead. Convince me."

"I tell my father I've gotten some illness. Nothing so serious he'd fly over to check on me, but something that would prevent me from getting on a plane. A terrible cold-flu thing involving my ears would be perfect."

"That sounds real medical," said Prudence, a schoolteacher, and therefore, far too practical in Vanessa's opinion. "What makes you think he'll believe that you happened to get a 'cold-flu thing' just when you're supposed to fly home to see Sebastian? You don't think he'll get suspicious?"

"Not if I have a physician speak to him."

"How will you manage that?"

Vanessa frowned a moment before the answer came to her. "I could hire someone. This city is full of actors."

"Okay, let's say for the sake of argument you do convince your father. What does that get you? You'd have to stay in your suite pretending to be sick."

"Not if I can convince my lady-in-waiting to help me, and I'm sure I can do that." The enthusiasm in Vanessa's voice increased as she saw her plan taking shape.

"Vanessa, you can't just go off on your own in New York City." Prudence sounded concerned. "You're a princess. You need security of some sort."

"Which brings us back to calling in the Marines as you put it. Or one Marine in particular. So what do you think?"

Prudence paused for a moment before saying, "I think I've got just the Marine for the job."

"I knew I could count on you. I have to get out of here, or I swear I'll go crazy!" Vanessa's voice was unsteady.

"You just stay put," Prudence said firmly. "Help is on the way."

Swaying with exhaustion, Vanessa headed straight for bed. She really didn't feel well. Maybe it was the rubbery chicken served at tonight's banquet dinner. Or the fact that she hadn't eaten much in days. Her unhappiness with her life had grown to such monumental proportions that she couldn't eat or sleep even when she had the time to, which wasn't very often.

She left a trail of clothing as she aimed for her bed like a battered fighter headed for a safe corner in the boxing ring. Crawling under the covers, she instantly fell asleep plotting her escape.

She woke early the next morning just as the sun was rising. Her body was still beat, but her mind kept racing, preventing her from getting more rest. She needed to perfect her plan. How should she get an actor to pose as a doctor? She'd met George Clooney in Cannes at the film festival last year, maybe he'd be willing to do it for her. He'd sounded so doctorly on that TV show.

Sliding on her silk robe with the royal coat of arms on the breast pocket, she headed for the bathroom, still groggy after only a handful of hours' sleep.

Opening the door, she was stunned to find U.S. Marine Captain Mark Wilder standing there waiting for her, wearing black jeans and a black T-shirt and looking incredibly dangerous and sexy. "You rang, Princess?" he drawled.

Mark couldn't believe he was stuck baby-sitting his sister-in-law's friend. So what if she was a princess?

He could have said no, he supposed. But Prudence had sounded so frantic and then his brother Joe had gotten on the line, and the next thing Mark knew, he'd agreed to fly up here to New York City to rescue Vanessa.

The ironic thing was that half an hour later he'd been ordered by his commanding officer to do the very same thing—to provide protection and security, among other things, for said princess. Without her knowledge of the true purpose of his mission.

While briefing him, his commanding officer had provided an entirely different picture of Princess Vanessa Alexandria Maria Teresa Von Volzemburg. Spoiled rich girl bored with her fancy life. She was driving her devoted father, who happened to be a valuable U.S. ally, crazy.

At the moment, Mark could see how she could easily drive a guy crazy. She looked great wearing a purple silk robe that showed plenty of cleavage. The last time he'd seen her, she'd been wearing a bridesmaid dress at Prudence and Joe's wedding nine months ago. He'd noticed her then. But she hadn't seemed to notice him, going out of her way to be friendly to everyone else attending that wedding while totally ignoring him.

Her behavior had irked him, Mark was willing to admit that. When he'd first seen her, he'd immediately noted Vanessa's resemblance to Grace Kelly—the same cool blond looks, same regal bearing. But Vanessa possessed exotically tilted eyes that flashed with green fire. And her lips weren't classy, they were downright lush and full. She had the kind of mouth that made a guy think wicked thoughts and the kind of body that did the same.

She wasn't model skinny. She definitely had curves. In all the right places. He liked that in a woman. He wasn't so sure he liked it in a princess. Made her too damn tempting.

"What are you doing in my bathroom?" she demanded, her voice an expression of picture-perfect princess outrage. Even her bare toes, painted pink, were curled in a display of feminine affront.

Mark couldn't believe he'd attended Marine Corps Officer Candidate School to end up here—playing bodyguard to a princess. The things he did for his family. And his country.

"You want me to leave?" He moved as if to depart.

She reached out a hand to halt him. "No, I...you just surprised me, that's all."

"Didn't Prudence tell you I was coming?"

"She told me she had a Marine in mind, yes. I just didn't expect you here so quickly. Or to find you in here." She waved a hand around the elegantly designed bathroom. "How did you get in without my security guard seeing you?"

"I'm an officer in the United States Marine Corps.

I've also trained with Force Recon, the Marines' elite reconnaissance unit," he informed her. "I know how to avoid detection, Princess."

"I want you to treat me normally," she told him, but in a princess-to-peon tone of voice that irked him no end. "You may call me Vanessa."

"And you may call me Captain," he retorted.

"I shall call you Mark," she stated, ignoring his sarcastic comment. "How much did Prudence tell you?"

"That you had some harebrained idea about running loose in the Big Apple."

"I sincerely doubt she worded it like that."

Mark shrugged, drawing her attention to his broad shoulders. "The bottom line is the same."

"You don't sound very approving."

"Like I said, I think it's a harebrained idea."

"Then why are you here?"

"Because I owe my brother a favor, and he asked me to help out." That was one reason.

"Your brother is a kind man." Her inference that Mark was not kind was clear.

"Yeah, Joe is a real peach," Mark mockingly agreed. "So let me get this straight. You want to take a little time off from your day job of princessing to trip the light fantastic, is that it?"

"That's one way of putting it, I suppose. May we continue this conversation in the other room?" she requested, drawing the lapels of her robe more closely together. "I'm not accustomed to having a discussion in the bathroom."

"I'd rather stay put for the time being." He flipped the toilet seat down, and gestured for her to sit there. "It seems only right that the throne be yours."

She frowned at him and then grinned. "You have a

wicked sense of humor, Captain. I like that in a Marine."

"And you have a wicked pair of legs, Vanessa. I like that in a princess."

"I'm so relieved to hear it," she noted wryly before elegantly sitting on the closed toilet seat as if it were indeed the intricately carved and jewel-encrusted royal throne of Volzemburg. "I certainly wouldn't want to destroy any of your misguided preconceptions about princesses."

"You've already done that by wanting to run away," he told her. "How hard can this princess gig be?"

"Hard enough," Vanessa replied in a tough voice coated with classy silk.

"Seems like it would be a cushy job to me," Mark noted, perching on the edge of the marble tub. "I'll bet a night in this place costs more than I make in a week, maybe even in a month."

"You're probably right. I don't know about the cost. The royal accountants take care of that sort of thing," she said with a wave of her hand.

"And what sort of thing are you looking for *me* to take care of?"

"Security," she immediately replied. "Mine, to be more precise. I'll pay you for your time, of course."

"Don't insult me," he stated curtly.

She blinked at him. "I wasn't trying to...."

"I'm doing this for Prudence." And because he'd been ordered to. "I'm on leave and had some time." He was *supposed* to be on leave, but it was cancelled when he'd gotten this assignment.

"I don't know what to say."

"There's no need to say anything. Now what's your plan?"

Vanessa repeated it to him just as she had to Prudence, only with more precision and firmness so he wouldn't think she hadn't thought things through.

"Sounds pretty lame to me. You hire some actor to pretend to be a doctor, and afterward he goes on to sell his story to the *National Tattler*." Noting the dark circles under her eyes and the paleness of her skin, he said, "I know a real doctor who'll recommend that you stay in bed and rest. Suffering from exhaustion is the term most frequently used."

"The Von Volzemburgs never suffer from exhaustion." The silky steeliness had returned to her voice. "We fought off Alexander the Great to protect our country and have been ruling ever since."

"That may be, but you don't have to pour hot oil over the castle battlements to protect your country any longer."

"No, now I just have to spend twenty hours a day going from reception to reception," she said tartly.

Mark flashed her a mocking smile and showed no pity. "Like I said, a real tough life. Too much partying. Too little sleep. Dr. Rosenthal is your man. He's seen it all before."

"He's never seen me before," she stated with haughty regality. "What makes you think he'd be willing to call my father?"

"He's a former Marine. Royalty doesn't scare him."

"Royalty doesn't scare you either, does it," she noted.

"You've got that right."

"Does anything frighten you?"

"Like I said, I'm a U.S. Marine Corps officer. We don't scare easily."

"Do you scare at all?"

"Well, ma'am," he drawled, "the idea of marriage and being committed to just one woman scares me."

"Marriage scares me, too," she surprised him by admitting.

"Since I'm not looking to marry you and you're not looking to marry me, neither one of us has anything to worry about then."

"Except getting caught," she said.

"Marines don't get caught. Now let's get back to your plan."

"Before we do that, I must insist that you come up with another diagnosis. My father will simply not accept that I'm suffering from exhaustion. That is not a suitable excuse to avoid returning home. No, the diagnosis must have something to do with my ears."

His gaze automatically traveled across her high cheekbones to her ears. They were dainty and feminine, and she wore an earring in each lobe. No cubic zirconias for this princess. No, those rocks were diamonds. "Are you supposed to sleep with those things in your ears?"

She touched her earlobe self-consciously. "I was too tired to do more than remove my clothing last night."

Which meant what? That she was naked beneath that silky purple robe?

Years of training allowed Mark to keep an impassive look on his face, but inside he was responding to her proximity like a male, not a Marine.

"Would your Dr. Rosenthal be willing to tell my father I can't fly because I have a cold-flu thing?" she asked. "Remember it has to involve my ears so that I wouldn't be able to fly for several days."

"Right. I'm sure the good doctor will say whatever is required."

"He won't have ethical problems with that?"

Mark wasn't about to go into Dr. Rosenthal's reasons for going along with this plan. "He's a friend. I already told you, he'll do as we ask. Let's move on. Where do you plan on sleeping at night?" he asked.

That was one question she hadn't yet considered. "Here, I suppose," she replied.

"Here in your suite?" He shook his head. "Not a good idea. You'd be going past your own security guard every night. Eventually you'd get caught."

"Fine. Then I'll sleep elsewhere. There are plenty of hotel rooms available in this city."

"Not that I can afford."

"I shall, of course, pay for all expenses," she loftily informed him.

"With what?" he demanded, pinning her with his saberlike gaze. "You think you're not going to draw attention to yourself by using your platinum princess credit card? Or did you plan on having your accountants come trailing after you to pay for things?"

"All right." She shot him an irritated look. "So I haven't exactly worked out all the details yet."

"Then it's a good thing that I have. But before we go any further, Princess, we need to get a few things clear. First off, I'm in charge of this op."

"Op?" she repeated with a lift of one of her delicately shaped eyebrows.

"Operation."

"Ah, a military rather than medical term, I'm assuming?" she noted mockingly.

"Affirmative. I've had more experience at this sort of thing than you have."

"At pretending to be a regular person?"

"At pretending to be something I'm not," Mark replied, very well aware of the fact that if Princess Vanessa Alexandria Maria Teresa Von Volzemburg knew the *real* reason he was here, she'd toss him out on his ear. It was his job to make sure she didn't find out.

Chapter Two

"Your Highness?" Vanessa's lady-in-waiting knocked on the bedroom door. "Are you ready for breakfast?"

"No, Celeste!" Vanessa jumped up and hurried out of the bathroom. Putting one hand on the door to prevent the other woman from entering, she added, "Come back in fifteen minutes, please."

"As Your Highness wishes."

Turning, Vanessa almost bumped into Mark. He moved so fast and so silently that she hadn't even realized he'd left the bathroom. She took a startled step backward and tripped over the hem of her robe.

Mark immediately reached out to steady her. She was standing so close to him now that she could see her own reflection in his blue eyes. Her heart skipped a beat.

His hands had automatically gone to her waist to steady her, and the feel of his strong hands warmed her through the silk of her robe. Indeed, she was all too conscious of each individual fingertip pressing against her, creating a restless stirring in the innermost recesses of her heart.

She could feel his heat, could sense the strength in his powerful body. She remembered the last time she'd seen him, at Prudence's wedding, where she noticed the swagger and confidence that was so much a part of him. Even standing still, as he was now, he still exuded a don't-mess-with-me hardness combined with a sexy bad-boy charm. What a potent combination.

But she was no wide-eyed military groupie to be taken in by a man in a uniform, or in this case a pair of jeans and a T-shirt. Especially one as sure of himself as Captain Mark Wilder was.

Even so, there was definitely something about this man that got to her.

As if suddenly realizing he'd been holding her long after she'd regained her balance, Mark abruptly released her and said, "Who is Celeste?"

Vanessa had to think a moment, so scattered were her thoughts from his proximity. "Celeste? She's my lady-in-waiting. She also serves as my private secretary." Vanessa quickly moved around him to walk to the middle of the bedroom. She needed a bit more space between them in order to regain her composure. Her body was still humming from his touch. "I have to have Celeste's help to pull this off."

Mark shook his head. "Not a good idea."

"Why not? Celeste can be trusted. You have your Marine comrades, I have my lady-in-waiting."

Mark rolled his eyes. He had lovely blue eyes, but it was his smile that was a real killer. Or maybe his blue eyes made his smile more powerful because his eyes gleamed with wicked humor. They weren't gleaming now, but they had when they'd been in the bathroom together. Now he was looking at her with impatience.

She was not the least bit intimidated. "I told you in the beginning when I outlined my plan to you that Celeste will cover my disappearance from the suite by acting as if I was still here."

"Fine. Get her in here, and I'll listen in to your explanation from the bathroom. I don't want her walking in and screaming because she finds a strange man in your bedroom."

"She wouldn't scream," Vanessa said.

"Why?" He pinned her with his gaze. "Because she's used to finding strange men in your bedroom?"

Vanessa bestowed a royal glare upon him. "That is a totally inappropriate question."

"Not when I'm providing your security, it's not. If there are any besotted beaux in the picture..."

"There aren't," she said curtly. Sebastian was hardly besotted with her. Besides he was back in Volzemburg.

"Good." Mark sounded entirely too satisfied with her response. "That simplifies things. Go ahead and call in your lady-in-whatever."

"Lady-in-waiting."

"Meanwhile, I'll call the doctor and have him come over here." Mark disappeared into the bathroom.

The man had no manners. Didn't he know it was rude to leave her presence without bowing first? Not a nose-to-the-floor kind of bow, but a respectful tilt of the head. Granted she'd told him to treat her normally, but then signs of respect from men were how she was normally treated. She'd have to learn to be more casual. But first she had to convince Celeste to help her.

She called the other woman in.

"Have I done something to offend you, Your Highness?'' Celeste asked in a nervous voice, looking at her with big brown eyes. Her dark hair was smoothed into place with a silver hair clip in a demure style that accentuated her round face.

"On the contrary," Vanessa reassured her, closing the bedroom door. "I need your assistance in a matter of great importance. This can be trusted to no one else but you. You know that these past few months have been very busy and, well…I'll simply be blunt with you, Celeste. I need some time away."

Celeste nodded solemnly. "I know. And I agree, Your Highness. Which is why I'm so glad we'll be returning to Volzemburg later today."

"No, we won't. We're staying here in New York a little longer." Vanessa quickly outlined her plan and Celeste's part in it.

"Your Highness, are you sure this is a good idea?" Celeste inquired in an extremely doubtful voice.

"I'm certain." Vanessa used her most regal tone, the one that could convince people that the sun was the moon. "Now, are you with me on this?"

Celeste nodded. "You know I'll do whatever you want me to, Your Highness. You've been so good to me and to my family. There were others who wanted this position, but you chose me, and I appreciate that more than I can say."

"I knew I could count on you."

"You are certain that you will never be in any danger?" Celeste asked. "I wouldn't be able to live with myself were anything to happen to you."

"I'll make sure nothing happens to her," Mark said from the bathroom doorway.

"Don't be alarmed," Vanessa said. "This is Captain Mark Wilder. He's my best friend's brother-in-law and a Marine. He'll be my temporary bodyguard. United States Marines guard the White House and the U.S. embassies. I'll be as safe as could be."

"What about Anton?" Celeste inquired.

"Anton, the royal security officer?" Vanessa noted the shine in her young lady-in-waiting's eyes. "The one who has an affection for you?"

Celeste blushed. "Anton would never do anything to compromise your safety," she said earnestly. "His first loyalty is to you and the Crown."

"His first loyalty is to my father," Vanessa noted bluntly, "which is why we're not telling Anton about this plan. He'd report it to the king in a flash. You must swear to me that you won't say a word to Anton."

"I swear, Your Highness." Celeste placed her hand on her own heart as she made the solemn vow. "You can trust me."

"Good. Then let's get this plan started. Tell Anton that I'm not feeling well this morning and that I don't wish to be disturbed. Oh, and when a Dr. Rosenthal arrives, please show him right in."

Celeste departed, leaving behind the breakfast she'd brought with her. Mark was already lifting the heavy silver covers from the plates. "I'm starving. Fruit. Is that all you eat for breakfast? Ah, pancakes." He licked his lips and dipped a finger into the small sterling pitcher that held warmed maple syrup. "Good. You don't mind if I eat some of this, do you?" He dragged an armchair over to the small table holding the food. "All I got on the red-eye flight up here was a bag of salty peanuts."

"Where did you fly in from?"

"Washington, D.C."

"Is that where you're stationed?"

He nodded and took a healthy bite of pancakes.

"A lovely place," she noted. "But I believe New York is my favorite American city. There's such an excitement here, you can almost hear its heartbeat."

"All I hear is traffic."

The man had no soul. Which wasn't surprising. Marines weren't known for their poetic natures.

Sitting there in her bedroom, eating her breakfast, he looked tough and sexy. The black T-shirt and black jeans he wore added a dangerous edge to his appearance. She could easily imagine him in an undercover operation. She could easily imagine him under her covers, period.

Oh my. She hadn't had these kinds of fantasies about a man in ages. Not since the last time she'd seen him at Prudence's wedding. This was certainly not the man to have those kinds of fantasies about. He was much too rough and too irreverent, too physical and too earthy. The qualifications for a good temporary bodyguard were not the same as those for a partner in a romantic relationship. Especially for a princess.

She wasn't looking for a man in her life. She was looking for some freedom.

Briskly shoving her erotic thoughts aside, she said, "While you're eating, I think I'll write up a list of what I'd like to accomplish during these next few days."

"Write away," he mumbled around a mouthful of pancake.

Taking a piece of official stationery from her personal supply on the Chippendale-style writing desk, she nibbled on the edge of a pen that had been given to her by the queen of England for her twenty-first birthday. "Despite all my visits to New York, I've never seen the major tourist attractions like the Statue of Liberty or the

Empire State Building.'' She wrote those down. Despite her best efforts, her handwriting had never been as elegant and flowing as her younger sister Anna's. A handwriting analyst had once done an article about Vanessa, saying she had a stubborn individual style that occasionally showed a surprising lack of confidence. Bingo. That was her personality in a nutshell. For once, the press got it right. ''Oh, and I'd love to take a moonlit stroll through Central Park.''

''Dumb move,'' he said bluntly.

She fixed him with a mocking stare. ''Come now, Mark, don't be shy. Tell me how you *really* feel.''

''Feelings have nothing to do with it.'' He took a sip of coffee. ''I'm telling you that walking through Central Park at night isn't smart.''

''Nonsense. I'll have a big strong Marine next to me. Besides, I've heard that New York is a much safer city now than it used to be.''

''You're going through all this trouble just so you can do touristy stuff, like visit the Statue of Liberty. That's all?'' This assignment might not be so hard after all, he decided, aside from the walk in the park. That was a definite no-go. He was not compromising her security to that extreme.

Protecting foreign dignitaries usually did not fall under his command, or any Marine's command for that matter, but this situation was unique. He'd been given this assignment because of his connections to Vanessa. As his C.O., his commanding officer, had told him, he was the only man for the job.

''I want to do what normal people do,'' Vanessa was saying. ''Eat at a fast-food restaurant, shop at a regular department store, go out dancing at a club at night— one that's not just for the rich and famous.''

Shopping. Mark froze, his fork poised above the next portion of pancake. He'd rather do a month of Arctic training than shop. Marines didn't shop. They went into a store, procured their necessities and got out ASAP.

And what had she listed before shopping? Dancing? He wasn't a big fan of that wimpy activity either. Unless it was line dancing. He'd mastered that at a nifty little bar called Buck's several years back. Where had that been? He frowned. So many assignments, so many bases.

But none of them had prepared him for dealing with a princess. If he had food like this served to him on a silver platter every day, he doubted he'd take off the way she wanted to. But then his mission was not to wonder why, his was to do or die.

And while the thought of dancing and shopping made him cringe, it wouldn't literally kill him. Not like his time spent in Desert Storm eleven years ago as a young recruit or his last overseas assignment a year ago. Those had been dangerous. This was a piece of cake.

He was a "Mustang," an enlisted man who'd worked his way up the ranks to become an officer. He thrived on challenges and was trained for efficiency. He excelled at strategy, and his strategy in this op was simple—to befriend Vanessa. A friendly princess was a more docile princess. He didn't want a rowdy royal on his hands here.

"There, my preliminary list is done. I think I'll go take a shower and get dressed now," she announced.

"Put on some exercise clothes," he told her, his thoughts already moving on to the next step in his plan.

She looked at him blankly. "Exercise clothes?"

"Yes, ma'am. Shorts and a T-shirt. Something like that."

"I don't own anything like that. I do have a dance leotard."

"I guess that will have to do." He wasn't quite sure exactly what a dance leotard looked like, but surely it was like something the women wore in a gym. "Put that on."

"Why?"

"Because I'm going to show you some moves."

"Dance moves?" she asked.

Mark shuddered. "Not in this lifetime."

"Then what?"

Instead of answering, he said, "Get in that shower and get changed. We don't have all day."

Twenty minutes later she stood on the bathroom threshold and announced, "I'm ready."

Mark turned. He wasn't ready for the slam of awareness that hit him midsection. The black leotard fit her like a second skin, outlining the curve of her breasts. She even had black ballet slippers on her dainty feet.

She looked ready for a performance of *Swan Lake,* not the mini–boot camp he had planned for her.

"Right." He had to pause and clear his throat. It felt as if he'd swallowed his tongue when he'd first seen her. "Okay, Princess—"

"I told you to call me Vanessa," she reminded him, gliding over to him.

Where did she learn to walk like that? he wondered irritably. *In princess school?*

Whatever lessons she'd learned in her royal life, he was about to teach her some hard facts. Life was tough. She had to be tougher.

He didn't have much time to bring her up to scratch.

First he had to assess her physical fitness.

"How many push-ups can you do?" he barked out.

She was clearly startled by his question. "I have no idea."

"How fast can you run a mile?" Her blank look was answer enough. "What about your exercise routine?" he continued. "Don't you have a personal trainer or something?"

"I'm too busy for that sort of thing," she said with a little wave of her hand.

"Too busy doing your princess thing," he scoffed. "Right. Well, let me warn you, Princess, those Cinderella glass slippers of yours are liable to get broken in the real world. And you've got to be prepared for that. Now sit down and put your elbow on this table."

"One does not put one's elbows on a table," she informed him before sitting down.

"One does if one is arm wrestling. Here, put your elbow on the table and bend your arm like this." He showed her. "Now grip my hand and try to push my arm over."

She frowned. "Why would I want to do that?"

"To show me how strong you are."

"Why do I have to be strong? I thought that was your job."

"I might need you as backup," he said mockingly.

She took him seriously. "Oh, I see." She blinked at him and leaned forward, thereby revealing an awesome amount of cleavage.

While his eyes were glued to her breasts, she adroitly shoved his arm almost to the table before he realized what she was up to. The little tease!

He recovered quickly and had her arm down in a flash. Tugging her to her feet a moment later, he began his next spiel. "I plan on teaching you some basic self-defense moves. If someone should grab you from behind like this—'' He put his arms around Vanessa, pinning her arms to her sides. ''I'm going to show you how you should respond.'' He released her to move in front of her. ''Now you put your arms around me as I just did you.''

She did as he ordered.

A thrill of forbidden excitement shot through her. Royal protocol precluded a princess from getting up close and personal with a U.S. Marine. Or with any other man, for that matter, unless his bloodlines were as pedigreed as her own and the man had been approved by her father.

Once, back when she was three or four, she'd left the opening of a new school in her country's capital city of St. Kristoff where she'd been expected to stand still like a dutiful little princess. But she'd sneaked off to the playground where the other children had been playing tag. She'd envied the children their laughter and had wanted to join in the fun.

Instead, she'd stumbled over her own feet and had tumbled into the grass.

Looking up, she'd seen her father standing in the doorway to the school, a frown and a look of intense disappointment on his face.

''Stand up and stop being such a wild child,'' he'd ordered her. ''A princess never cries.''

She'd tried for years not to disappoint him, but had never quite succeeded in silencing that secret inner little girl that wanted to play tag. The truth was, she was still a wild child at heart. And standing there with her arms around Mark made her feel gloriously alive for the first time in years.

Unaware of the memories streaking through her mind, Mark continued giving orders in his brisk Marine voice. "There are several ways to respond to an attack from the rear like this. You can stomp your attacker's foot. You can perform a shin scrape with the heel of your shoe. Or you can bend your knee for a backward kick to the groin with your heel. Do you understand those moves?"

"Yes." She understood them but was distracted by her body pressed against his, spoon fashion. She was tall for a princess. The term *gangly* had been applied to her more than once. "Vertical Vanessa" was another one the European tabloids had used. But Mark was taller by several inches. He had to be over six foot.

While she was debating his height, Mark was moving on to the next segment. "Most attacks against women come from the front. Either the choke or the slap. To protect yourself from the slap, you put your forearm up like this." He illustrated. "Now put your hands around my throat as if you were going to choke me."

When she hesitated, he said, "Just think how aggravated you were with me when I called your plans lame."

Nodding, she reached out. His skin was warm beneath her fingers. She could feel his Adam's apple against her thumbs.

"The proper response to a choke hold is to push your attacker's pinkies away from you," he said, bending her fingers back, gently enough not to hurt her but firmly enough for her to see how such a move done vigorously would cause a surprising amount of pain.

"Think you got that?" he asked.

"Yes." She'd also gotten all hot and bothered by all this close body contact. Her cheeks felt flushed, and her forehead was damp with sweat. A princess was never allowed to sweat. Not even on a state visit to India in a hundred-and-ten-degree heat. She'd almost passed out on that visit, but she hadn't. And she hadn't visibly sweated. Until now.

Excitement shot through her, heating her skin wherever they touched. A new kind of chemistry sizzled between them, a male-female chemistry that was sexy and intense.

"Good."

"Mmm, good." She had no idea what he was talking about. She felt all dreamy and distracted.

"But sometimes, Princess—" He snared her in his arms, flashed a devilishly sexy smile at her and then lowered his head until his lips almost brushed hers as he spoke. "Sometimes your attacker might use a more devious approach. Will you be prepared for that? Will you be prepared for this?"

Before she could think, his mouth captured hers.

Chapter Three

Vanessa was held captive. Not by the strength of his arms, but by the intensity of his passion...and her own.

She returned Mark's kiss with a spirit of hunger that surprised them both. His lips moved over hers with an ever-fluid interplay that stole her breath away and vanquished all logic. Instead, she was consumed by a blind yearning that made her immediate world slide into oblivion. He made her shiver and burn at the same time, provoking a sensual response she could neither understand nor control.

The thin material of her leotard and his black T-shirt provided little protection against the earthy warmth of his body. His hands slid down her spine to the small of her back to tug her close, binding her to him. The passage of his hands created a new flame in the fire burning within her.

Mark parted his legs to brace himself as she melted against him. His action intensified the intimacy of their embrace, added a new level of heated friction.

Tunneling his hand beneath the golden tumble of her hair, he lured her to part her lips even farther for him. She eagerly complied. He rewarded her by doing enticing things with his tongue, moves that made Vanessa's knees weak and her body throb. Her tongue answered his as his mouth slanted across hers in a new angle that afforded them both even more erotic pleasure.

Mark's hands slid with deft sureness over her derriere, pulling her deeper into the kiss, into the madness. In his arms she was a different person. She was female to his bold male. She felt the thrust of his arousal, and her body responded with a receptive aching need to draw him to her. She was both the conquered and the conqueror.

And then it was all over.

Shocked, she swayed before him as Mark took several steps back. She felt naked without his arms around her.

"You weren't supposed to kiss me back!" Mark growled, shooting her a look that was downright accusatory. "You should have used one of the self-defense techniques I just showed you instead of melting in my arms."

Passion quickly dissolved in a sea of humiliation. Red-hot embarrassment rolled over her like a tidal wave. So did red-hot anger, making Vanessa react without thinking.

Enlisting a speedy move of her own, she took hold of his arm and twisted her hips, and presto—gravity took over, knocking a startled Mark completely off balance. A second later he was falling to the floor, landing on his sexy denim-clad derriere in the middle of the Aubusson carpet.

At that precise moment, Celeste opened the bedroom

door and ushered in Dr. Rosenthal, who viewed Mark with a wide grin.

"I've heard of bowing to royalty, Wilder, but never thought I'd see the day when a woman would set you on your keister."

"The captain was showing me his moves, so I showed him one of mine," Vanessa said in a demure voice.

"I didn't teach you that move," Mark growled accusingly at Vanessa even as he leaped to his feet with the grace of a cat. A big cat, something in the angry-tiger family. A lesser woman would have taken a step back.

But Vanessa was a princess, and years of training helped her keep her cool.

"No, you didn't teach me that move. Olga did."

"Who the hell is Olga?" Mark demanded.

"She was the East German Olympic fencing champion for five straight years in the 1980s. Now she teaches fencing in Volzemburg. Over the years, she's given me a few pointers in self-defense."

"You could have told me that."

"You could have asked me," she retorted.

"Children, children, enough squabbling," Dr. Rosenthal said. "As fascinating as this may be, I do have patients waiting for me back at my office." The doctor looked more like a young John Wayne than George Clooney. He had a rugged face and direct demeanor, but kind brown eyes. "You're looking flushed, Princess Vanessa. I fear you may have a fever."

"Brain fever," Mark muttered under his breath.

"Thank you, Celeste, you may leave us now," Vanessa informed her wide-eyed lady-in-waiting.

The doctor opened his black bag and removed a stethoscope.

"I'm not sure what Mark told you," she began, eyeing his medical bag warily.

"Relax, Princess," Mark drawled. "He's not going to draw too much blood."

"I'm not going to draw any blood," Dr. Rosenthal assured her with a reprimanding look in Mark's direction. "You two are doing enough of that on your own."

"I apologize, Dr. Rosenthal," Vanessa said. "It's very kind of you to take the time off from your busy practice to come here today."

"The doc owes me a favor," Mark said.

"I want to check you out a bit before I call your father," Dr. Rosenthal said. "Make sure nothing really is wrong with you."

"Aside from a stubborn nature, you mean."

She ignored Mark's comment.

"Take a deep breath. Hold it. Let it out."

"Have you known Mark long?" she asked.

"Long enough," the doctor replied, taking a wooden tongue depressor out of his bag. "Open your mouth and go ah." Shining a tiny high-intensity flashlight in her mouth, he noted, "Looks good. How long have you known Mark, Your Highness?"

"His brother, Joe, married my best friend Prudence."

"Ah, Joe." Dr. Rosenthal nodded as he tossed the tongue depressor in a ritzy garbage can with the royal seal on it. "The charmer in the Wilder family."

"And Mark?" Vanessa asked. "What's he?"

"The proud one," Dr. Rosenthal instantly replied.

"Really? Why's that? Because he's a Marine?"

"Don't you have someplace else to be, Doc?" Mark

said, clearly uncomfortable with the direction this conversation was taking.

"The doctor has to phone my father before he leaves," she reminded Mark.

"How much sleep have you been getting a night?" the doctor asked her.

"Four, maybe five hours, if I'm lucky," she replied.

"And your appetite?"

"He ate most of my breakfast," Vanessa noted with a regal tilt of her head in Mark's direction.

"Hey, there was enough on that platter to feed a family of five," Mark said in his own defense. "And she hardly touched any of it."

"Mmm. You do show signs of nervous exhaustion," Dr. Rosenthal told her. "All kidding aside, I do think a break would do you good."

"There, you see?" Vanessa shot Mark a triumphant look. "The doctor agrees with me."

Mark felt the first twinges of guilt tugging at his conscience. The good doctor was in on the plan, of course. A former Marine himself, Abraham Rosenthal hadn't asked any questions and had only been told information about Mark's mission on a need-to-know basis.

"Shall I call your father from my office or from the phone here?" the doctor asked.

"Here would be best, I believe," Vanessa replied. "What do you think, Mark?"

It was the first time she'd ever consulted his opinion on anything and Mark found that he liked the inquiring look she gave him, as if she cared what he replied. Which was ridiculous. She was used to giving orders as much as he was. She clearly wasn't a woman who kowtowed to others. She was a princess, for heaven's sake, nothing like the women he usually went for—the voluptuous cheerleader type.

Not that the cheerleaders were empty-headed—Cindy was a court stenographer, Rusti a telemarketer. And they hadn't been without class. But they'd been more interested in pleasing a man than in just about anything else.

And Mark had loved that about them. Well, not *love*. He didn't do love.

When he eventually did marry, it would be to a woman who understood the demands of a career Marine officer. Plenty of women were impressed by the uniform, but not many were willing to stick around for the life-style. His older brother, Justice, was a prime example of that. He'd married his high-school sweetheart right after entering the Marine Corps at age eighteen only to have her divorce him a short while later.

Joe had married a woman accustomed to the life of a Marine. After all, Prudence's father was a sergeant major. But Joe claimed that it hadn't helped his case any.

Mark only knew that he planned on doing his family proud. As the only one who'd chosen the career path of a commissioned officer, he had a responsibility to his father to prove that he could rise to the highest ranks in the corps. The right kind of wife would help in that quest, someone quiet and not too demanding.

A princess definitely wouldn't do. Way too high maintenance.

But, damn, she kissed better than any cheerleader he'd ever met.

Where the heck had a princess like her learned to kiss like that?

"Mark?" Vanessa said. "You didn't answer my

question. Do you think the doctor should phone my father from my room here at the hotel?''

"Affirmative,'' Mark replied in his best crisp military voice.

"Remember, I don't want to alarm my father into sending the royal physician over to check me out, I only want to delay my return home a few days.''

"He knows the drill,'' Mark assured her, nodding at Abraham. And he did. He did his part with admirable alacrity.

"Well?'' Vanessa asked nervously as the doctor hung up the phone from his transatlantic call.

"Enjoy your time off,'' Abraham told Vanessa. "You heard me tell your father that you have laryngitis as well as a sinus infection with ocular involvement. He agreed that it would be best if you stayed where you are for the time being. I said it would take a week before you'd be safe to fly.''

"Thank you!'' Vanessa looked as if she wanted to throw her arms around the good doctor and hug him, but instead she held out her hand for a formal handshake.

"Your father said if you're not better in a week he'll send the royal physician and come to New York himself,'' the doctor warned her. "You're going to have to check in with him in a few days. And I'm to give him an update tomorrow.''

Vanessa looked worried. "Will that be a problem for you?''

"No. Not as long as Mark keeps me informed on your health.''

"I'll make sure she gets plenty of rest,'' Mark said. Eyeing them both in exasperation, she reminded them, "Gentlemen, the point of this entire exercise is for me to get some freedom, not some rest."

"See you get both," Dr. Rosenthal ordered before letting himself out.

"You're going to need different clothes," Mark said. They were the first words he'd spoken since Dr. Rosenthal had departed five minutes ago. She would have suspected he was pouting about her having dumped him on his too sexy fanny earlier, but Prudence had once told her that Marines never pout. They get even.

Which, honestly, did make Vanessa just a tad nervous. But it also excited her. The prospect of matching wits with Mark had her blood racing.

"You'll need a disguise, so no one will recognize you," he was saying.

"I'll be sure to leave my tiara here," she noted mockingly.

"You do that. Do you own any jeans? I already know you don't own any T-shirts."

"I'm sure they sell T-shirts in the hotel gift shop."

"Fine. Have Celeste play tourist and go down and buy one for you."

"An excellent idea. And one I'd actually already thought of myself," she added.

"Sure you say that now..."

"A Von Volzemburg never lies," she loftily informed him.

"This from a woman who just told a huge whopper to her own father."

A woman. He'd just referred to her as a woman instead of a princess. A small thing, no doubt, but it felt huge in her own mind. Vanessa hugged the idea of Mark thinking of her as a woman instead of a princess.

Goodness knew he'd kissed her the way a man kissed a woman. There had been nothing cordial or formal about the meeting of their lips. It had been sexy and exhilarating, passionate and intense. It had been better than the best chocolate ever concocted by the royal chocolatier—and that was saying something!

Vanessa considered herself something of a connoisseur where chocolate was concerned. But she was a novice at male-female relationships. Which was ridiculous for a woman her age. She was almost thirty, for heaven's sake. But the rules for her code of behavior were much stricter than they were for anyone else. She'd led a sheltered upbringing to put it mildly.

"As I was saying, a Von Volzemburg never lies, unless they are fighting for their freedom. Back in 1456, King Frederick put a mark on the castle saying that it was infected with the plague. It kept the enemy forces away, and the castle survived."

"Well, you're not going to survive the streets of New York City if you don't fit in," he warned her.

"I understand perfectly."

Half an hour later, Mark stared at her in disbelief. "I thought you said you understood the concept of a disguise. Those tight-fitting jeans are sure to catch the attention of every male under the age of eighty!"

She blushed. Okay, so the jeans were tight. She'd borrowed them from Celeste, who had no derriere at all to speak of. Now Mark made her feel like a stuffed sausage in the jeans.

Sending a scorching look his way, she grabbed another outfit from the closet and marched back to the bathroom. This time he couldn't complain about the fit of her slacks. The Valentino haute couture black pantsuit had been hand tailored to her body. The understated elegance made it a perfect fit with the silk chartreuse blouse.

Opening the door, she posed against the doorway with chic nonchalance.

Mark was clearly not impressed. "Why don't you just put a sign around your neck saying I'm A Rich Princess, Kidnap Me."

This Marine was *really* starting to aggravate her now. "What kind of disguise are you proposing? Marx Brothers glasses and a mustache? Perhaps you'd like me to wear a Charlie Chaplin costume and swing a cane around?"

"Nothing that drastic will be required, although you are getting a little closer to what I'm aiming for here. Tone down the sex appeal."

"I beg your pardon?"

"You heard me. Tone down the sex appeal."

"I'll have you know that this suit was designed by Valentino."

"I don't care if it was designed by the pope, it makes you look too..." He made a motion with his hands.

Was that some kind of Marine sign language? "Too what?"

"Too good. Tone down your looks. Here, while you were in the bathroom I checked in my bag. I've got some sweats you can borrow."

"Sweats?" she repeated as if he'd said a dirty word.

"Sweatpants and a sweatshirt." He held them out for her. They were navy blue. Seeing that she made no effort to take them from him, he added, "They're clean. I washed them before I packed them."

"How reassuring. What's that lump on the sweatshirt?"

"It's a hood. We'll put a baseball cap on your head,

maybe add a flannel shirt, and presto, you're no longer a princess.''

"No, I'm dressed like a bum."

"Listen, Princess, we're not aiming for any fashion awards," he growled. "Our goal is to get out of here without being noticed."

"And you don't think someone dressed so disreputably in such an elite hotel isn't going to garner attention?"

She had a point. Mark wasn't pleased to have to admit that. He hadn't been thinking clearly since he'd seen her in those skintight jeans. "All right. So wear the jeans and the T-shirt Celeste got from the gift shop."

"You said I looked fat in those jeans."

He gave her a startled look. "I did not."

"You said, and I quote you here, that the jeans were 'tight fitting.'"

"Yeah. So?"

"So that means I'm too fat for them."

He rolled his eyes. "It means that you looked too good in them."

"That's not how it sounded to me."

"Look, I'm not going to stand here and debate the issue with you." He tossed the discarded T-shirt at her. "Put this back on along with the jeans and this sweatshirt. And tuck your hair under this Yankees baseball cap."

"You're a baseball fan?"

"Of course. I suppose you prefer cricket or polo maybe?"

"Actually I love basketball, but the NBA hasn't been the same since Michael Jordan retired." She had the pleasure of seeing his startled expression before she closed the bathroom door.

Vanessa did the best she could with what she had in hand. She'd discarded her jewelry but felt naked with nothing around her neck, so she put on the St. Christopher medal her mother had given her when she was a child. Studying her reflection in the mirror, she didn't recognize herself. Which was a good thing, right? Anton, her security guard, wouldn't recognize her either then.

Vanessa definitely wouldn't win any fashion contests. She'd deliberately omitted her normal beauty routine and had opted for a natural-colored lipstick as her only makeup.

Opening the bathroom door, she informed Mark, "This is my final outfit. I'm not changing clothes again."

"You'll do." Holding out his hand, he said, "Let's go. I believe you mentioned something about a fast-food restaurant on that list of yours. You feel like eating tacos or burgers?"

"What about clothes? I can't walk out of here with the things on my back and nothing else."

His hand dropped to his side and his mocking smile returned. "Of course you can't. Why don't we pack up the royal luggage, and then we'll go to Burger King?"

"Stop making fun of me."

"Then stop being ridiculous. I already put some of your stuff in my bag. The more you carry the harder it is to slip out unnoticed."

"You touched my things?"

She made him sound like a pervert who'd been pawing through her lingerie drawer. He was just following orders here. "Look, all I did was take some necessary items of clothing."

"Show me."

"Fine." He yanked the zip open on his duffel bag and showed her what he'd packed.

"That won't do." She pulled out the sheer pink underwear and silk shirt. Marching over to the dresser, she proceeded to select other lingerie.

"We don't have all day," he growled.

She hesitated, still distracted by the thought of him touching her most intimate apparel. The image made her hot all over.

In the end, Vanessa wasn't sure what she stuffed into his duffel bag, it certainly wasn't much. Some sensible underwear, a few tops. She decided she could buy the rest. She had some American money with her.

"Are you ready, Princess?" he inquired mockingly.

"Yes, Captain, I am. Are you?"

"A Marine is always ready for whatever comes," Mark automatically stated, but inside he was thinking that this mission was already turning out to be far more complicated than he'd anticipated.

Chapter Four

"Now what?" Vanessa whispered as she stood beside him next to the door leading from her bedroom to the hotel hallway. "Do you have a plan?"

"Of course I have a plan. I'm a Marine Corps officer. That's what we do. Plan."

"So what is the plan?"

"While you were getting dressed, I asked Celeste to order lunch for you. Room service should be coming along anytime now...."

"Actually the food is cooked by the royal chef in the hotel kitchen, and then a valet from the royal household brings up the meal. It's royal protocol. To prevent anyone from tampering with the food."

"What, no royal taster?"

He was half kidding but she replied, "He stays with my father at all times and doesn't travel with me."

Boy, did she live in a different universe than he did. Cracking open the door just a tad, Mark looked down the hallway. The elevator doors opened.

"Ah, here he comes. Get ready to move on my command." Carefully closing the door, he waited as the valet went past that doorway to the main door leading to the elaborate suite. That's where Anton was stationed. From there the royal guard had a clear view down both sides of the hallway. "We need to slip out while Anton's attention is on that valet. Celeste said she'd distract him. I sure hope we can trust her."

"I trust her with my life," Vanessa said.

Mark wasn't accustomed to trusting anyone other than a fellow Marine with his life. Sure he'd trust his own family, but they were all Marines, too. "Let's go." He hurried her through the door and down the hallway to the elevator.

Vanessa's heart beat faster as adrenaline flew through her body. She was doing it, she was making her great escape! Her adventure was about to begin. She couldn't wait.

Her hand was clasped in Mark's as he kept their pace leisurely and deliberate. Running down the hall was sure to garner unwanted attention.

Never had a hallway seemed so long. Finally they reached the elevator doors. Vanessa tried not to grin like a fool. Freedom. She could almost taste it.

Eyeing the reflection in the mirrored panel above the elevator's call button, Mark suddenly swore under his breath and tugged her into his arms.

"Play along with me," he whispered urgently, his lips almost touching hers. "Anton is watching us. I have to kiss you, so pretend you're hot for me and kiss me back."

Vanessa was about to tell him that there was no way Anton could possibly recognize her in the ridiculous outfit she was in—with a baseball cap and sweatshirt hood on her head—when Mark's mouth covered hers and captured her mumbled protest.

Mark continued the kiss even as he backed her through the open doors into the waiting elevator. The minute the elevator doors closed, he quickly ended the kiss. Looking around, he whispered, "We're clear."

There might not be anyone else in the elevator, but they certainly were not clear. Vanessa felt anything but *clear.* She felt completely befuddled and definitely irritated at his ability to kiss her one minute and toss her aside the next. Who did he think he was to treat her this way?

Before she could voice her complaints, Mark put a finger to her mouth. Leaning close again, he whispered, "Elevator has surveillance cameras. Keep your head down and don't say anything."

He'd put a baseball cap on his own head, the brim tugged low to cover more of his face. It was amazing that he'd been able to kiss her at all without the stiffened brims of their caps getting in the way. The man obviously had experience kissing in all kinds of situations.

Draping an arm around her, Mark guided her through the busy lobby and out onto the street, where he turned right and headed away from Central Park at a brisk pace matched by the other New Yorkers on the sidewalk. Vanessa was breathless by the time they paused in front of a fast-food restaurant several long blocks away. She'd lost track of how many turns they'd made, but she hadn't forgotten her irritation with him.

She didn't forget it...until he ushered her into the restaurant, and she smelled it—freshly made fries. Then everything else was erased as her mouth watered and her stomach growled.

Standing in front of the stainless-steel counter, she looked up at the photographs of the selections in awe. What should she have? So many choices. She definitely wanted fries, so she told the perky young teenager, "I'll have a large order of fries."

"Is that all?"

"No. I want…" She stared at the items offered and couldn't decide. They had chicken sandwiches, salads, hamburgers, ribs, fish sandwiches. Okay, not a salad. But did she want chicken or beef? Or fish?

"Hurry it up," Vanessa heard a man growl. It took her a moment to realize it wasn't Mark who was complaining.

Slinging his duffel bag over one shoulder, Mark hurriedly placed his order and added, "She'll have a double-deluxe cheeseburger meal number four."

"Maybe I want chicken," she protested.

"And maybe you want to start a riot," Mark quietly warned her. "There's a huge line behind you."

"Here's your change, sir," the teenager said.

"Thanks." Grabbing their tray filled with food, Mark hustled her toward an empty booth in the corner.

Ignoring him totally once they sat down, she focused her attention on her meal, gobbling a handful of French fries in the first two seconds. She closed her eyes in delight. Ah, heaven. Sheer heaven.

Sure, while in America, she'd sometimes sent Celeste out to get her fries, but by the time she brought them back to the hotel they'd gone cold and lacked this just-out-of-the-oil taste that was so addictive. Vanessa had even tried getting her limo to stop yesterday and have Celeste run in to pick up fries, but the driver had refused, saying her father had forbidden such behavior because it was not deemed befitting of a royal princess.

"Look, we're going to have to get a few things clear," Mark began after she'd made some headway on her cheeseburger.

"I agree." She gave him a haughty stare, not easy to do when she'd just wiped mustard from her chin and had to look at him from under the stupid bill of her cap. "For one thing, it's very rude to order for me without consulting me."

"You were standing there as if you'd never been in a place like this before."

"Which I haven't. That's why I wanted to come here."

He frowned. "I thought you went to school in America."

"Only for one year, and I wasn't allowed off-campus."

"Sounds like boot camp. Minus the weapons."

She had to smile. "The only weapons we had were the pancakes Mrs. Manly cooked up in the cafeteria every Sunday. They made great Frisbees."

"What was Prudence doing in a ritzy boarding school in the first place? Her dad's a Marine."

"She was there on a partial scholarship, and her father sent her as a form of discipline." She nibbled on another fry. "We met and became friends."

Tearing his gaze away from her lips, he spoke in a curt voice. "As I was saying, you can't create a scene like you almost did by holding up the ordering line that way. It makes you stand out like a sore thumb."

Her smile disappeared. Being likened to a sore thumb did not amuse Vanessa. No one had ever dared to speak to her in such a manner. Even at school, she'd been treated with deference and respect, even when she was being disciplined for some escapade. And since then, she'd been a working princess, traveling the world on behalf of her country. She was not a sore thumb.

Suddenly she wasn't as hungry as she'd been. Putting her burger back down, she nibbled on a French fry.

"Finish your food," Mark said.

"We definitely need to clear some things up," Vanessa stated, straightening her shoulders and tilting her head back to bestow another regal stare upon him. The darn billed cap made it hard for her to see anything above chest level, but she didn't dare remove it for fear of being recognized. All she'd need was for some paparazzi to snap her picture, and the jig would be up.

"It is not your place to order me around. If I choose not to eat, then I won't eat. If I choose to take time over selecting my lunch, I shall do so. That does not mean I am a sore thumb. If I make a few missteps, you may politely guide me. But you are merely giving me direction, not issuing an order. Besides, I find your orders to be extremely contradictory."

Now that she'd taken the edge off her hunger, her earlier irritation at his actions back at the hotel returned tenfold. "Earlier today you told me not to kiss you back, then a short time later you told me to kiss you as if I was 'hot for you,' I believe is the way you so elegantly put it. I would suggest that you make up your mind one way or the other."

"I only kissed you because Anton was looking our way."

She gritted her teeth. Could the man be any more insulting? He was as good as telling her that he'd kissed her under duress. How was that supposed to make her feel? Infuriated, that's how it made her feel. And strangely bereft.

"You've made it perfectly clear that you didn't kiss

me because you wanted to, there's no need to repeat yourself on that matter. I only kissed you back out of curiosity the first time, and the second time because, as you said, Anton was watching us. But I suggest that there not be a third time where kissing is concerned. In Volzemburg we have an old saying 'Third time watch out.' Now if you are done eating, and it looks like you are, judging by the empty tray, then I suggest we move on. There are people waiting to sit, and I certainly wouldn't want to hold them up and stand out like a sore thumb,'' she noted tartly.

Women! Slinging his duffel bag over his shoulder, Mark dumped the paper wrappers from their lunch into the trash. He'd never had trouble figuring them out before, but then this woman was a princess. He might not be quite as much of a ladies' man as his younger brother, Joe, but he'd had more than his fair share of success with the female sex.

And while it was true that Mark had told her not to kiss him and then had reversed that order a short time later, that didn't mean that his strategy was faulty. He had to remind himself of the real goal of his mission.

The trouble with that was that she got to him. As a woman not as a princess.

Dressed as she was in casual clothing, Mark could almost imagine that Vanessa was a tourist out to see New York City. But then she'd tilt her head a certain way, as if she was more accustomed to wearing a tiara than a baseball cap. Which was no doubt true. That knowledge didn't stop him from wanting to kiss her again, however.

Which went beyond foolish and fell into the downright-stupid arena.

* * *

Vanessa hated her disguise. The jeans were extremely tight now that she'd eaten, and they made her feel fat. And the sweatshirt may have been washed, but it still smelled like Mark, which kept reminding her of being held close in his arms.

Salvation was across the street. A large well-known discount department store. What she needed was a makeover. She'd already gone from princess to bum, now she needed to go from bum to regular American woman.

"Hey, where are you going?" Mark demanded as she made a beeline toward the street.

"Shopping."

His stomach turned. "Now?"

"Yes, now."

"We can't cross here," he stated, taking her by the arm as if fearing she'd make a dash for it. "We have to go to the corner. We don't need you getting a jay-walking ticket."

"We certainly don't," Vanessa agreed, casting a cautious look at a fierce-looking policewoman who was checking parking meters and giving out tickets.

"Okay, here's the plan for shopping," Mark began as they joined a group of pedestrians waiting for the light to turn green.

He was interrupted by Vanessa, who said, "I don't want to hear about any more plans. I just want to go shopping and have fun."

"You tell him, girlfriend," a young woman with an elaborate cornrow hairdo said from beside them.

A man on the other side of them said, "Yo, man, you got a right to be the boss."

Luckily the light turned green before any further debate could ensue.

Once the group had gone on to cross the street, Vanessa turned to him and said, "See what you started?"

"Me? You're the one."

"Come on—" she tugged on his arm "—before the light turns red."

He was seeing red. How could one woman be so much trouble?

Blithely unaware of his thoughts, Vanessa hurried to the store like a kid racing to see what Santa had left her under the tree Christmas morning. He'd expected more of a stiff-upper-lip attitude from her, not this show of excitement and enjoyment. When she'd closed her eyes and moaned over a French fry, he'd almost moaned himself. She'd looked like a woman in the throes of passion. And she'd kissed that way, too. Totally immersed in the moment.

He needed to remind himself that she got just as excited about fries or shopping. He was nothing special here.

But Vanessa, well, she was something else. And she was heading for the door without waiting for him. He had to hurry to catch up with her, the strap of his duffel bag digging into his shoulder.

"I've always wanted to come to a place like this," she confessed as he held the door open for her. "Thank you." She paused inside to simply gaze around and soak everything in.

Whenever she went into a store, everyone else was locked out. The only people around were those intended to serve her every need. Did she want a drink? Was this chair comfortable enough? Models would parade a designer's latest couture outfits for her perusal.

She'd never been surrounded by other shoppers before. They all seemed to know where they were going.

The teenage boy in black leather with a nose ring, his girlfriend in matching attire and nose ring, the woman pushing a stroller with a toddler crying—they all moved with utter confidence like ants in an anthill, scurrying about with a definite purpose in mind.

How nice it must be to be so sure of yourself, of your life, to know where you were going rather than just following orders. How rewarding it must be to have goals of your own rather than living your life to please others.

"Seen enough?" Mark asked. "Ready to leave now?"

"We just got here."

"Funny," he muttered. "It already feels like we've been here for ages."

"Surely a big bad Marine like you isn't afraid of a little shopping," she teased him.

"It wasn't exactly part of my officer training," he retorted.

"A pity. I guess we'll just have to learn as we go along."

"Hold on." Grabbing her arm, he stopped her from taking off down the main aisle. "We have to stay together."

"Fine." She paused in front of a sign listing various department locations. "I'm going up to the women's department."

"You want more clothes? You don't have enough already?"

Vanessa sighed. "You don't have any sisters, do you."

"What's that got to do with anything?"

"If you had sisters, you'd be more accustomed to a female's point of view."

"Hey, I've had plenty of experience with females," Mark retorted.

"Really." She gave him a doubtful look. "I find that hard to believe. Now your brother Joe, he's the charmer in your family."

"All the Wilder men have a way with women."

"And so modest, too," she noted dryly. "Come on, the women's department is upstairs." As they rode the escalator side by side, she confessed, "I've never actually bought anything on sale before. I'm looking forward to it."

She had that little-girl-at-Christmas look again, the one that Mark found so endearing. How did she manage to do that, go from regal to adorable in the blink of an eye? Was that part of being a princess or was it simply part of her personality?

Placing his duffel bag on the floor at his feet, he watched her as she headed for the nearby sale racks. Her green eyes were shining but the overhead fluorescent lighting leached some of the gold from her hair. She wasn't looking her best, if he was perfectly honest here, in that baseball cap and his bulky sweatshirt.

The strange thing was that he found her incredibly sexy anyway as she held a dress up to her body, wrapping an arm around the waist as she stared at herself in the mirror. The dress was light blue with little flowers on it, and it was short, well above the knee.

"What do you think?" she asked, turning for his opinion. "Would this look good on me?"

"Anything would look good on you," he replied without thinking.

She appeared surprised by his answer.

She wasn't the only one. What was he doing, talking like that? He couldn't afford to be flirting with her. "Go try it on," he ordered her. "There's a fitting room over there."

"I thought you said we had to stay together," she reminded him.

Right. Jeez, he wasn't thinking straight here. "Just buy it. If it doesn't fit you, too bad."

"Is that what American shoppers do?"

"If it doesn't fit they return it, but we're not going through that process." Shopping was bad enough, returning stuff was out of the question. He'd drawn his line in the shopping sand, and he wasn't crossing it.

"Okay," she said, so agreeable that he was immediately suspicious.

"Okay?" he repeated.

"Yes, okay. I think I'll get this dress too." She plucked a simple black cotton dress from the rack. "I can't believe the prices here." She moved to another sale rack and picked out a pair of jeans and a skirt. All the while Mark stood guard impatiently.

"Look, the point of this exercise is for me to enjoy shopping the way a regular American woman would. You're not making this a pleasant experience by breathing down my neck the way you are," she told him in exasperation.

"I can assure you that American women have to deal with impatient men all the time when they're shopping together."

"I bet most women leave the men at home," she said.

"Well, that's not possible in your case, so don't even think about it."

"Then stop sighing and glaring at your watch every second."

"Marines do not sigh."

"Grunt then. Whatever you call that noise, it's distracting me."

"Heaven forbid I distract you," he drawled, folding his arms over his chest.

Oh, he was distracting her all right. He was doing it now, his biceps straining against the sleeves of his black cotton T-shirt.

She looked away, but that didn't end things. He still had the power to make her heart skip. The truth was that even wearing his sweatshirt and baseball cap was getting to her.

Vanessa needed a new outfit—not princess attire, not borrowed garments, but something of her *own*. Something that had nothing to do with her position.

She wanted to shed that persona along with the mismatched clothes and let the new Vanessa appear, like a butterfly emerging from a cocoon. And that's how she felt, as if she'd been locked in a cocoon. Only, Vanessa's cocoon was made of glass and had all the world looking in as she went through her changes.

From the time she'd been a small child, the paparazzi had watched her every move and commented on everything from her hair and her gangly height to her clothes and her weight. That kind of constant critical inspection had turned her into an approval-seeking machine from a very young age. But she'd never quite learned how to gain that approval.

Sometimes she thought she began disappointing her father the second she was born. He'd wanted a son. He'd gotten her instead.

Things had gotten worse since her mother's death. Her mother had acted as a buffer. Vanessa had barely turned sixteen when her mother died in a car crash.

There never is a good time to lose a parent, but Vanessa had been particularly vulnerable as a late-blooming gawky teenager who lacked her mother's grace and style. Whenever her father had criticized her, her mother had always managed to say something to soothe the hurt. Vanessa still missed her intensely.

Since then she felt as if her every move was being dissected under a microscope, and she was constantly found lacking by her father.

Vanessa shook off the melancholy such thoughts always brought her. She was here, in a department store in the middle of New York, free to do as she chose for the first time in her life. She needed to enjoy this moment.

"Are you done yet?" Mark demanded in an aggravated voice.

Suddenly Mark represented the male dominance she'd had to suffer through because of her father. She was tired of pleasing. She was tired of a man telling her what to do, of a man trying to drain her pleasure by laying on guilt.

"No, I'm not done yet." She deliberately walked through the neighboring intimate apparel section, hoping to make Mark even more uncomfortable. He grabbed his duffel bag and came after her.

Glancing over her shoulder, she noticed that Mark's eyes were shifting from side to side and his jaw was clenching rather like a man forced to do girl stuff against his will. He bumped into her before realizing she'd paused in front of a display of lilac-colored bras and matching panties. He stared at the lacy bras and then at her.

To her surprise, his frazzled look was replaced with a heated gaze in her direction. "You'd look good in that color," Mark noted huskily.

Instead of him being the one discomfited, now she was the one blushing. He watched her with those impressive blue eyes of his, the slide of his eyes down her face and body like the brush of fingertips—tangible in their visual touch.

Her breath caught in her throat, and she was overcome with the awareness of the man standing so close beside her that she could almost hear his heartbeat. Twice today she'd been held in his arms and kissed until she could no longer tell up from down.

"Shoes," she muttered, trying to hang on to her composure. Breaking off eye contact, she noted, "I need a pair of sandals."

"We're not buying you a whole new wardrobe here," he warned her.

"I can't keep wearing these heavy walking shoes." She held out her foot and moved her ankle to show him what she meant. "It won't take me long."

"Yeah, right. Where have I heard that before?"

"I have no idea," she replied in a lofty tone. "You certainly haven't heard it from me."

"I certainly have. Several times. Back at the hotel when you were changing clothes."

"That delay was entirely your fault. You're the one who was unhappy with my attire."

"Are you going to buy the stuff you're holding in your arms?"

She had the items she'd collected all squashed against her body, as if they could provide some kind of protection from this powerful attraction between them.

"Yes, of course I am. I have some cash."

She had just enough left after making those purchases to buy sandals. Mark's long-suffering sighs seemed to arise every two seconds despite her best efforts to hurry.

Because of her borrowed tight-fitting jeans, she was having a hard time bending over to fasten the straps on the sandals she was trying on. She was wondering if perhaps she should stick with a slide style instead when Mark took matters into his own hands, literally. Bending on one knee, he took her foot in a firm but gentle hold as he slid the sandal into place and fastened it. His fingers were warm on her skin as they brushed against her ankle, creating a surge of awareness that zipped through her entire body.

"Look, Mommy, that man on his knees is proposing!" a little girl exclaimed.

Mark and Vanessa both froze in place. Their eyes met and held. Vanessa barely realized that the girl had come over to put her sticky hands on her knee. All she could think of was the concept of Mark proposing to her.

The girl's harried mother quickly joined them, breaking the moment. "Don't touch!" she scolded her daughter. "Sorry about that," she told Vanessa. "Ever since she saw my brother on his knees proposing to his sweetheart a few weeks ago, she thinks any man on bended knee is proposing."

Mark quickly leaped to his feet as Vanessa said, "That's all right. No harm done. Right, Mark?"

"Affirmative." He still looked a little shaken to her eyes, however.

She quickly decided to get the shoes she was wearing and made her purchase in the shoe department. They placed the shoes she had been wearing in a bag for her. Accustomed as she was to others doing her carrying for her, she left that bag and the larger one with the clothing she'd bought earlier at the cashier's desk as she turned away to pocket her meager change. Sure enough, Mark picked the paper bags up for her. He carried them over

to where she stood and then dumped them at her feet.
"These are yours."

"I know that." Placing the smaller shoe bag into the
larger one, she gamely picked it up.

The store had gotten much more crowded while she'd
been searching for the perfect sandal.

Mark noticed the increasing crowd as well. "Stay
close to me," he ordered her.

Easy for him to say. He was powerfully built and
carrying a huge duffel bag. While Vanessa was taller
than many of the women around her, many of them had
Olga's hefty build and looked as though they could have
taken on the entire East German fencing team themselves.

It happened in the blink of an eye. The crowd spilled
out from the aisles and suddenly Vanessa was swept up
in it as the rush of humanity surged forward. Carried
along by the crowd, she became separated from Mark
as she struggled to maintain possession of her large
shopping bag.

Shrieks from excited shoppers made her ears ring as
the stampede continued. It wasn't until Vanessa almost
knocked over a mannequin wearing a wedding dress
that she realized she was in the bridal department. Huge
banners hung from the walls, proclaiming, Bridal Bo-
nanza Sale: One Hour Only!

Vanessa tried to work her way toward the outer walls,
but she was hemmed in by women determined to find
a bargain. Fear welled up inside her. She'd never experienced anything like this.

Then out of the blue, she was plucked from the
crowd, the comforting safety of Mark's arm guiding her
through the chaos. It seemed to take forever to get out

of the melee. But held tucked against him, her earlier fear was gone.

It wasn't until they were on the escalator heading back downstairs and away from the marital mayhem that Mark spoke. "I told you I hated shopping," he growled.

"Are stores like this all the time?"

"Like I'd know," he retorted, keeping his arm around her as they descended to the main floor.

"The shops are closed for me when I go shopping."

"A princess perk, huh?"

She nodded.

"Sounds like one you should keep," Mark noted dryly before holding the door open for her.

Out on the street, he wasted no time in hailing a cab.

"Where are we going now?" she asked as he hustled her inside so fast she almost lost her baseball cap.

"This time I'm calling the shots." Mark gave an address to the cabbie before continuing to speak to her. "I think we've had enough excitement for one day, don't you?"

Vanessa nodded. Being a regular person was more work than she'd expected.

Chapter Five

"Where are we?" Vanessa asked as the cab pulled up in front of a brownstone in a quiet neighborhood.

"Home," Mark replied, opening the cab door and helping her out.

She tried to ignore the feel of his warm hand holding hers, but it was impossible. Each time he touched her she experienced an increasingly powerful jolt of awareness. This wasn't something she'd experienced before. In the course of her work, she met a number of men, shook their hands, or even had her hand kissed. None of them had ever had this effect on her.

Certainly Sebastian had never had this effect on her. He was like a brother to her, which is why the thought of marrying him made her stomach clench. Over the past year, she'd tried to talk to her father about her feelings, tried to prevent him from insisting that Sebastian be her husband. But her words fell on deaf ears. Her father already knew what he thought, he didn't care what *she* thought. He was the king and her father, and he knew what was best.

Her stomach clenched again.

Vanessa took a series of calming breaths, reminding herself that she was temporarily free of her father's domination. But the ties that bound her to him weren't just those of a princess loyal to her king and the throne, they were of a daughter who'd spent much of her life trying to please a father but rarely succeeding. Marrying Sebastian would please her father, but this time she had to draw the line.

There was no point dwelling on all that now, however. She had more immediate issues. She waited until the cab had pulled away before demanding more information. "What do you mean by home?"

"An old buddy of mine is loaning me his place for a few days. I decided it would be safer to stay here than at a hotel where someone might recognize you. Not to mention it being easier on the budget. Come on," he said, holding the building's wrought-iron door open for her. "His place is on the third floor."

Vanessa was out of breath by the time they reached the apartment. Mark, meanwhile, acted as if he could race up another twenty flights of stairs without breaking a sweat. He fished a key out of his jean pocket, which drew the black denim more tautly across the most intimate part of his body.

She hurriedly looked away. A lady didn't look there.

One day out of royal captivity, and she'd turned into a rowdy woman. She wasn't sure whether to be pleased…or alarmed.

Mark opened the door and ushered her inside. Vanessa quickly focused her attention on her surroundings rather than Mark's sexy anatomy. The apartment's living room was small and simply furnished with a couch, coffee table and a huge TV-and-stereo combination. The kitchen opened off to one side and included the basics—stove, sink, fridge. Down the hallway was a bathroom that would have fit in the smallest broom closet in the palace back home. Only at the end of her tour did she realize that there was only one bedroom, only one king-size bed with a mirrored headboard and a leopard-print cover on it.

She turned a suspicious gaze in Mark's direction.

"Hey, I plan on sleeping on the couch in the living room," he assured her, his hands held palm out as if warding off any protest she might make. "Your reputation is safe with me, Princess."

"I have a name, and I prefer you use it."

"Vanessa." He rolled it off his tongue.

She shivered, even though she was hot, not cold. Very hot. Center-of-the-sun kind of hot.

It was a warm May day, and the sun was shining on the roof directly above them. That must be why she felt so warm. That and the fact that she was still wearing Mark's sweatshirt.

She quickly peeled it off. Her baseball cap came off with it.

Now she was wearing a baggy I Love New York T-shirt over the too-tight jeans she'd borrowed. Quickly running her fingers through her hair, she knew the royal hairdresser would be outraged at the tumbled state of her hair.

Of course the hairdresser's outrage was the least of her problems. Vanessa's father was the one she had to watch out for. "I need to check in with Celeste," she said.

"Use my cell phone and don't talk for long," he told her.

"Why? Do you think my father has had the phones bugged?"

Mark already knew that the answer was yes. That's why he was here. Because her father had learned of Vanessa's phone call to Prudence.

He'd never participated in an operation where his loyalty was anything but one hundred ten percent to the Marine Corps and his objectives. But for the first time in his life, he felt that loyalty wavering a bit.

He was just following orders here, he reminded himself. The deception was necessary for him to carry out his orders.

So why did he feel lower than a snake's belly when she looked at him with those gorgeous green eyes of hers as if she trusted him with her life? In effect, she *was* trusting him with her life. She was doing that because he was Prudence's brother-in-law, because he was a Marine.

And as a Marine, honor and loyalty were critical things with him. The bottom line was that he felt dishonorable having to lie to her.

But his orders were clear. She couldn't know the truth.

"This is America, we don't bug phones here for no reason," he said. "Your father may be powerful in Volzemburg, but here..." He shrugged, communicating one thing while he thought another. The king was powerful enough to have gotten Mark embroiled in this sticky situation. His C.O. had made it clear that should Mark successfully complete this operation, his career would be headed for the fast track to promotion.

"If you don't think my father is bugging my phone,

why do you want me to use your cell phone?'' Vanessa asked.

"Because my friend had his phone service disconnected while he's overseas. And I don't want you talking long because it's expensive.''

"Oh. Okay, then. I won't be long.''

Her trusting acceptance of his answer made him feel even worse. He'd told her the truth, or part of it. His friend *had* had the phone service disconnected. But he'd lent Mark this apartment at the Marine Corps' request.

Mark didn't know if Vanessa's security officer, Anton, was in on the king's hidden agenda. That's the reason he didn't want her talking long. Mark had a feeling the king's plan was to have as few insiders know about this situation as possible. The king wanted his daughter to think she had a few days of freedom, to get it "out of her system'' was the way it was presented to him, while keeping her within his watch.

And Mark was the watcher. The spy, the one reporting back to the king directly via nightly e-mail reports.

He hadn't become an officer in the U.S. Marine Corps to participate in this kind of subterfuge. Not that he wasn't good at it. During his time with Force Recon he'd done his fair share of undercover operations. But those had involved national security and protection of the interests of the United States. Not playing bodyguard to a spoiled princess.

The thing was, she wasn't as spoiled as he'd expected. His job would be a lot easier if she was simply a bored rich girl. Then this guilt starting to nag him would disappear.

But no, she had to be more complicated than that. She had to moan in delight over the taste of French fries. She had to lead him into the temptation of a department store's lingerie department and flirt with him over a sexy lilac bra. She had to smile at the little girl in the shoe department who'd run up to her and put her sticky fingers all over Vanessa's knee while she had been trying on sandals.

Mark was trained to observe the little things, and there were things about Vanessa that told him there was more to her than met the eye. Not that what met the eye wasn't unexpectedly sexy.

He refocused his attention on her conversation with Celeste. As promised, Vanessa kept it short. When she hung up, he said, "Well?"

Vanessa smiled. "Everything is going according to plan."

Which was a good thing and should make him feel a lot better than he did.

Vanessa felt much better after she tried on all the new clothes she'd bought and found they all fit. She then went through the clothes she'd packed in Mark's duffel. He'd just dumped them on top of the bed, which quivered and moved when she sat on it. That startled her for a second until it registered that it was a water bed.

Her attention returned to the pile of clothing. Going through them, she found a pair of black knit pants she didn't know she'd included.

A minute later, she'd kicked off her shoes and discarded her too-tight jeans for the comfort of knit. "Ahhhh." She sighed with pleasure. Next the baggy T-shirt was replaced with a silk knit top in powder blue. Yes, that felt *soooo* much better.

All she needed was more French fries, and she would be in heaven. But wait, was that pizza she smelled?

Pizza would be good, she instantly decided. Not as good as French fries, but a close second.

She opened the bedroom door and looked down the hallway to the living room where Mark was setting a flat cardboard box on the coffee table.

"You hungry?" he asked as she walked into the room.

"Mmm, starving." She headed straight for the pizza.

"I had no idea princesses were such a hungry bunch," Mark teased her as she sat beside him and took a bite.

"Mmm." She closed her eyes as the pleasure of tomato sauce, cheese and sweet sausage bloomed in her mouth.

"They don't have pizza where you come from?"

"Not like this." She dabbed at her chin with a napkin he handed her. "Thanks."

"You're welcome. I just never expected a princess to show such passion for pizza."

"I suspect there's a great deal you never expected a princess to do. Like temporarily running away the way I have."

He shrugged, drawing her attention to the breadth of his shoulders.

"You have a lot to learn about princesses," she told him.

"Why don't you teach me."

"You make that sound like an order rather than a request."

"I'm a Marine," Mark said. "I'm used to giving orders."

"And used to having them obeyed, no doubt."

"Yes," he readily admitted. "Something wrong with that?"

''Only when you're not dealing with Marines. Is that why you aren't married?''

Mark almost choked on his pizza. ''Whaa...at?''

''You're older than Joe, yet you're not married.''

''So what? You're Prudence's age, and you're not married either. Why not?''

''Because I haven't found the right man. Marrying into royalty isn't exactly a simple matter.''

''Neither is marrying a Marine. Duty comes first.''

''Trust me, I know all about duty coming first. But duty won't keep you warm at night,'' she said wistfully.

''I can find someone to keep me warm at night without marrying them.''

''I can't,'' she said with simple candor. ''Definitely not allowed.''

''Princesses are supposed to remain pure, huh?''

She threw a crumpled-up napkin at him. ''Don't sound so sarcastic.''

''Pardon me, Princess.''

''I told you to call me Vanessa.''

They both reached for the same piece of pizza. She stubbornly refused to give up her claim to it. Her eyes met his as the battle silently continued. Then she grinned at him, distracting him enough for her to gain possession of the slice in question.

''Competitive little thing, aren't you?'' Mark noted ruefully.

She laughed. ''I'm hardly little. I used to wish I was petite like my mother and sister. But I'm not. The press calls me Vertical Vanessa because I'm so tall.''

''You seem just right to me.''

She paused, the pizza slice midway to her mouth to stare at him. ''I do?''

"Yeah." He nodded as if disconcerted by his own words.

"Thank you," she said softly.

"You're welcome."

They ate in silence for a while. But her mind was moving a mile a minute, processing what he'd said. *Just right.* No one had ever said that to her before. She'd always been *too* something—too exuberant, too willful, too tall, too heavy, too much. Never just right. His words made her heart glow like a sunset in St. Kristoff.

She wanted to know more about the man who made her feel this way. But she didn't want to blurt out any more personal questions, like asking him why he hadn't married. So she said, "Have you ever been to New York before?"

He nodded. "A couple of times."

"What are your favorite places?"

Mark considered her question carefully. He'd already said more than he meant to by telling her he thought she was just right. He needed to keep the conversation on a more impersonal level. Favorite places was a move in the right direction.

Now he needed an appropriate answer. There was a little strip club down in the Lower East Side he and a bunch of his fellow Marines once frequented, but he doubted she'd want to hear about that. Even if she did, he wasn't about to tell her.

Or there was a jazz club in Harlem. No, not her style probably. "I like the Met," he finally said.

"The art museum?"

"Yeah," Mark said defensively. "Something wrong with that?"

"No, it's just that…"

"You thought I was a dumb Marine who didn't know a van Gogh from a hole in the wall."

"I'm just surprised by your answer, that's all."

"There's also a great strip club I've visited once or twice," he drawled, wanting to shock her now. "Does that surprise you?"

"Yes, it does. I wouldn't think a good-looking man like you would have to pay to see a woman undress."

Mark blinked at her. That wasn't what he'd expected her to say. And judging by the startled look on her face, he was willing to bet she hadn't expected to say that either.

"So you think I'm good-looking, huh? That's nice to know."

"I'm so glad to have made your day, Captain." Her voice mocked him.

"You've certainly made it a memorable day. So what's it really like, being a princess? What's a normal day in your life like?"

"A normal day? I'm not sure my life is normal at all. In fact, I'm sure it isn't. That's one of the reasons I wanted to get away. Have you ever felt like there was something more to life, something you were missing out on?"

He shrugged.

"Well, I've felt that way for years now," she murmured, her expression pensive. "As if I'm shutting off the best parts of myself—the creative, expressive parts—in order to fit in."

"You didn't seem to have any trouble expressing yourself with me."

"That's because I was already breaking free of the chains of duty and loyalty that were killing me. Killing my soul, anyway."

Mark told himself she was just being melodramatic. How could the pampered life she led kill her soul? "Millions of women would give anything to be in your shoes."

"Then they're welcome to my shoes, all two hundred pairs of them."

"A budding Mrs. Marcos, huh?"

"Actually it's part of the uniform." She remembered how great he'd looked in his dress blues uniform at Prudence's wedding. "I have a dresser who is in charge of my wardrobe. She selected and packed everything for this trip. She keeps detailed records, on a computer no less, of each outfit. It wouldn't do for me to show up at the same charity event in the same gown two years in a row. So she keeps track of where I wore it, what shoes and gloves and hat go with it."

"Your baseball cap won't do, huh?"

She shook her head. "I've got fifty hats, forty cocktail dresses, one hundred and forty day suits. Then there are the twenty formal ball gowns. I only know the numbers because my dresser did an inventory right before I left." The trappings had only added to the weight of the burden she was already under. Because none of the clothes represented the real Vanessa, the one struggling to find herself. They were the wardrobe of a princess and despite a lifetime spent working at it, she still felt it was a role too big for her.

She'd been the cause of too many disappointments—from the fact that she'd been born a girl instead of the boy her father wanted to the fact that she refused to marry the man of her father's choice. In between those cornerstones were hundreds of small incidents, when she'd been too candid or too "natural" or too something her father didn't think was proper. She'd had to stomp out her true nature, and the effort of doing so was grinding her down until she felt utterly hollow and lonely inside.

Until today. Today was…special.

"So that's what your life is like, counting your ball gowns?" he teased her.

"My dresser does the counting." Vanessa reached for another slice of pizza. "As for a typical day, let's see." She paused to take a bite, daintily munching on it and swallowing before speaking again. "I'm usually out of the palace by seven. My work as a princess has three components—official engagements, charity projects and high ceremonies like Displaying the Colors. Of the three, I enjoy the charity work the most, but even there I have to be careful and follow protocol. I can't encroach on another royal family's territory, and I can't get involved in a charity that the palace considers to be controversial, like doing away with land mines, for example."

"Weapons of warfare are ugly but often necessary."

"We'll just have to agree to disagree on that," she said with a shake of her head.

"It wouldn't be the first thing we disagree on," Mark noted wryly.

"We agree on some things. For example, we both like pizza."

"And French fries."

"And French fries," she agreed. "Now, where was I…oh yes, my schedule as a princess. Well, for one thing, it's set a good six months in advance. As I said, I start my days usually around seven and make some appearances at a local hospital or factory or school. Then lunch usually includes a board meeting of some kind, I'm on fifteen different boards. A change of clothes, which often takes over an hour, and I'm off again maybe to give a speech or two. Celeste goes over the important elements with me, the important people I'll be meeting, their names, their spouses and children's names and ages, that sort of thing. After a full day's round of events, there is usually an evening function of some kind, which means a third change of clothing. The other night it was a charity auction and ball put on by the Chocolate Manufacturers Convention. My country is known for its chocolate, and some of the traveling I do is to promote that.''

"Sounds like a tough job,'' he said in a mocking voice.

His words irked her. "Many of the charities I'm involved with also require traveling to see things that would break your heart. I'm particularly interested in orphans and improving conditions of orphanages in Eastern Europe as well as the rest of the world. I've seen children in deplorable conditions.'' Her voice was so tight she couldn't go on.

One of the reasons her schedule was so full was that she took every opportunity to tell others about the need for help in places like Bosnia and Romania. To do that, she traveled extensively across Europe, America and Australia to spread the word. She was needed to open a new opera house in Kansas? Fine, she'd show up provided she could talk about what her father termed her "pet cause.''

Again she'd been a disappointment to him. He wanted her to get involved with delicate things like the Volzemburg Ballet or the Garden Society. Not the nitty-gritty world of children in dire need.

Vanessa longed to do more, but was testing her father's limits as it was. So she did what she could, and sometimes fell asleep with the faces of those children imprinted on her mind, bringing her tears and nightmares in the middle of the night.

"What would you do if you quit your princess job?" he asked.

"It's not the kind of job you get to quit. You're born into it, and you die in it."

"Sounds like the Marine Corps," he noted with a grin. "Here." He handed her a can of beer. "You sound like you could use a drink."

She opened the pop top and broke a nail doing so. "Is there a glass?"

He took a sip from his aluminum can before answering. "In the kitchen, I suppose. You should go get one."

She eyed him suspiciously. "So that you can grab that last piece of pizza? I think not. I can drink from the can."

Again they both simultaneously reached for the pizza slice. This time he was the one who flashed an endearingly boyish smile at her and she was the one who paused, just for a second, but it was enough for him to grab the slice.

"I was full anyway," she loftily informed him.

"Yeah, right," Mark scoffed.

"You know it just now occurs to me that at Prudence's wedding, all those Marines addressed every woman as "ma'am." You haven't done that with me."

"Because you're a princess. I figured you've been ma'amed enough in your lifetime."

She grinned at him. "You're right about that."

"What do you say we watch some TV?"

"That sounds fine," she replied, settling into a more comfortable position on the couch. Noting the way he was staring at her bare feet, she said, "You know, there was a time in my country's history when seeing a princess's bare feet without being married to said princess would result in your being thrown into the castle dungeon."

"How long ago was that rule in effect?" he cautiously asked as he reached for the remote control.

"You don't have to worry." She patted his arm reassuringly, very much aware of the warmth of his bare skin beneath her fingertips. Her fingers still hummed when she returned them to her lap. "I believe it stopped being enforced in the 1890s. Besides, this isn't the first time you've seen my bare feet," she reminded him. "You won't get thrown into the palace dungeon because you saw me without my glass slippers."

"That's a relief." He turned on the TV only to be stunned by the X-rated scene being shown.

"Your friend has interesting tastes in television programming," Vanessa noted dryly, before leaning forward to peer at the screen. "Is that whipping cream they're using?"

"I have no idea, and I don't aim on finding out," Mark said, hastily clicking on another channel.

"And just when things were getting interesting," she said with a grin, enjoying his discomfiture, as she had earlier at the department store.

"We can always turn back to that channel if you really want to see it," he said, challenging her.

"No, that's okay. This looks like the evening news. Wait a second, stay on that station. That's the department store we visited this afternoon!"

Vanessa's heart stopped. Had she been found out already?

Chapter Six

"Vanessa didn't even realize she was trembling until she grabbed hold of Mark's arm, needing something solid to hold on to as the room seemed to spin around her.

"This was ground zero for Marital Madness—the biggest bridal sale in the city. It only comes once a year and the shoppers race for the deals," the reporter said in her eager TV voice.

Film footage showed the mayhem. And there in the middle of it all was Vanessa. Well, not *her* exactly. Her Yankees baseball cap was all you could see. And Mark's back, his duffel bag slung over his shoulder.

"This couple seemed caught off guard by what was going on around them," the reporter said in a voice-over.

"You've got that right," Mark muttered, remembering the adrenaline shooting through his body when he'd lost sight of Vanessa. He hadn't felt that way since his earliest days in the Marines, when he'd been stationed in the Gulf.

Yes, he'd been caught off guard, all right. By a woman who adored French fries and knocked him for a loop with her kisses.

"Don't show our faces, please don't show our faces," Vanessa was whispering, her hold on his arm tightening.

"Hey, Princess, chill out," Mark teased her. He couldn't help himself. That was how he reacted when faced with fear. He used humor to defuse the situation.

Vanessa, however, didn't appear to appreciate his stress-management style. Drawing herself into what he called her "regal" mode, she stiffly removed her hand from his arm. He immediately missed the warmth of her fingers on his bare skin.

"I am perfectly chilled," she informed him.

Her voice was certainly chilly enough, it was darn right arctic.

"Look, they've gone on to another story," he said. "No one could have identified us from that brief shot of the back of our heads. It was a close call, however. I told you we shouldn't have gone shopping."

Vanessa might have let things slide, had he not added that last sentence. But there was no way she was letting that one go by unanswered. "You should have noticed that a camera crew was there. That's your job."

Her comment stung because he'd already thought of that fact himself. But aloud he said, "Sure, blame me."

"Why did you agree to do this job?" she bluntly demanded.

Mark deliberately kept his face impassive, but inside he froze. Had she somehow guessed what was really going on? No, she couldn't have.

"I agreed because Prudence asked me." *And because I was ordered to.* Suspecting that Vanessa would take off, King Leopold of Volzemburg had also suspected she'd contact her good friend Prudence and through her, one of the Wilders. That's why he'd bugged her phones at the hotel. The king was one step ahead of his rebellious daughter. Mark had been ordered to keep tabs on Vanessa and to report directly back to her father. Those orders came via Mark's C.O. from the highest members of the U.S. Government and the U.S. State Department.

"Sometimes you act as if you're here against your will." Her gaze was direct, daring him to lie to her.

"I'm a Marine," he reminded her. "I don't do anything against my will." Little could Mark know that his words would come back to haunt him one day soon.

"I still say that we should have watched the end of the Lakers game instead of the first inning of the baseball game," Vanessa said four hours later.

To which Mark replied, "You had the remote control."

He'd given it to her as a peace offering and they'd spent the past few hours channel surfing on cable TV.

"Let's see what else is on…" She flicked past CNN and a home shopping channel before stopping. "Ah, *Chocolat,*" she sighed. "One of my favorites."

"More food?" he groaned.

"No, *Chocolat* the movie." She pointed to the screen. "Haven't you seen this yet? It's wonderful."

Juliette Binoche radiated on the large TV screen. "She's a looker," Mark noted approvingly.

Did that mean he preferred brunettes to blondes? Vanessa wondered before becoming caught up again in the story of a woman showing up in a new town with the temptation of chocolate.

"Did all that chocolate make you homesick?" Mark asked when the movie ended.

She shook her head. But the love scenes with Johnny

Depp had vividly brought to mind the kisses she'd shared today with Mark.

And here she was, spending the night with him. Yes, he said he'd be sleeping out here on the couch and she'd be in the bedroom, but still…there was something inexplicably intimate about sharing the apartment with him. And watching that romantic movie with him had only increased her awareness of Mark and the situation they found themselves in.

Vanessa also loved the way Juliette Binoche's character learned to make her own path in life, and not merely to follow in her mother's footsteps. It was a message that spoke strongly to Vanessa's heart.

Her heart was vulnerable to Mark. How wonderful it would be if she were just a young woman working in New York, free to choose any man she desired. And heaven knew she desired Mark. How empowering it must be to have that kind of freedom.

Of course, the case could be made that as a princess she did have a certain amount of power of her own. A royal proclamation would not get Mark's attention, however. His friend, Dr. Rosenthal, had already told her that Mark was the proud one in his family. She could just imagine how he'd respond to being pursued by a princess.

Besides, Vanessa had her pride as well. Mark clearly had a certain amount of charm and confidence where women were concerned. She was not the first female to notice his dark blue eyes or powerfully built body. She probably was one of the few females to have knocked him on his derriere, however. That realization gave her pleasure.

"What are you smiling about?" Mark asked suspiciously.

"I was just remembering how I knocked you on your...keister."

"I fell down, you didn't knock me down."

"Fall down a lot do you?" she teased him.

"Only when you're around."

He was looking at her in a way that both disarmed and aroused her. She caught her breath at the flare of hunger reflected in his eyes. Did he look at every woman this way, or did this mean that he was experiencing the same attraction she was?

"You have a way of knocking a guy off balance," he murmured.

"I do?"

He nodded, his gaze lowering to her mouth. "Yes, you do."

"I wasn't aware of that." Was he remembering their kisses as she had? Did he want to kiss her again?

"Well, now you know."

"Why are we whispering?" she asked.

"Because then I have to lean closer to hear you."

"And that's a good thing?"

He shook his head, as if to clear his jumbled thoughts. "No," he ruefully acknowledged. "That's probably not a good thing." He reached across her for the remote and clicked off the television. "I think we've watched enough for one night."

She was tempted to watch him all night. And not just to watch him, but to kiss him, to feel his body close to hers.

Tomorrow was another day, she reminded herself. There was no need to do anything without thinking things through a bit first.

"Don't you have cable TV where you come from?" Mark was asking.

"When I'm traveling, I'm never in my hotel room

long enough to watch TV,'' Vanessa replied. "At home we have a few televisions in the palace, but none have cable. My father doesn't approve of the cultural influence and excessive violence of the American media. He thinks he can keep our country timeless like Camelot. He can't. The people of Volzemburg have satellite dishes on their homes. They get all these stations and I don't. You can't keep the world out.''

"Maybe your father is just trying to be protective.''

"*Overprotective* is more like it," she muttered.

"So you two never got along?''

"Having a king for a father makes for a strained relationship," she told him. "How about you?''

"My dad is a retired Marine, and I'm sure he believes that outranks a king.''

Vanessa had to laugh. "I remember your dad from Prudence's wedding. He seemed nice.''

"Nice?'' Now Mark was the one who laughed. "That's not how I'd describe him.''

"How would you describe him then?''

"Honest, blunt, dependable, loyal.''

"All admirable characteristics.''

"Yes, they are.''

"He must be proud that all his sons are Marines.''

"He wasn't thrilled with me becoming an officer," Mark admitted.

"Why not?''

He shrugged. "We come from a long line of enlisted men.''

"So? I would think that would make your accomplishments all the greater.''

"Not in my dad's eyes.''

"I know how that feels.'' Vanessa's eyes met his, her gaze filled with understanding. "Being judged by someone you love and coming up short. It hurts.''

She waited for him to brag that Marines don't get hurt, but he didn't make that claim. In fact, he just clammed up, as if regretting having said as much as he had. Sensing he wanted some space, she said good-night and retired to her bedroom. Before leaving the living room, she turned back to look at Mark over her shoulder, but he was already totally engrossed in a laptop computer he'd pulled from his duffel bag.

Mark thought about Vanessa's words all night as he tossed and turned on the couch. There was no way his dad had anything in common with King Leopold. Sure, maybe the two men were autocratic and used to getting their own way. But Mark's dad would never do the stuff the king had done to Vanessa, spying on her, belittling her.

So his dad had certain expectations where Mark was concerned. Bill Wilder had expectations for all his sons. There was nothing wrong with that. That's what a father did.

Yet Mark could still remember the look his dad had given him when he'd first told him his decision to apply to OCS, Officer Candidate School, in Quantico, Virginia. It hadn't been the look of a proud father. He'd appeared puzzled, maybe disappointed even.

And there had been the comments about Mark's latest tour of duty—a staff job with a general in Washington. His brothers had good-naturedly teased him about being a "staff weenie." Of course, he'd immediately had to wrestle them to the ground to prove his physical toughness.

But it irked him that he'd had to prove anything.

So he was a little less rough around the edges than his brothers. So he'd developed some social graces they lacked. So he wasn't pursuing an exciting combat command at the moment. He had a plan here.

Staff jobs were more advantageous to his military career in the long run. He'd worked with a special-warfare unit dedicated to combating terrorists. Rewarding work, yes. High adrenaline, for sure. Security had always been an area of special interest for him.

He was involved with security now, even if he was working at a staff job. This assignment with Vanessa could be considered a security operation. He had to keep her secure in order to keep the relations between the United States and Volzemburg smooth. And while it was true that a country whose major export was chocolate might not be a major ally at first glance, closer inspection showed that Volzemburg's geographical proximity to Eastern Europe made it important.

How had he gotten himself into such a sticky situation? He hadn't done it on his own, he'd been ordered into this mess.

Not that his orders included kissing Vanessa. The *princess*. He needed to keep thinking of her as the princess and not as Vanessa, a woman he was attracted to.

He was *not* attracted to her, he harshly ordered himself. And if said attraction did exist, it was to cease immediately. He could not allow himself to feel anything for her.

Maybe the urge to take her in his arms and kiss her again was due to the fact that he'd gone too long without a woman. That must be it. That had to be it. Anything else was unacceptable.

Mark sighed. This had all the makings of a very messy mission.

But then Mark didn't join the Marine Corps because he thought it was going to be easy. He expected it to be tough. No pain, no gain. Above all, you must never quit or give up.

Leadership was a critical part of being a Marine. And the ability of the corps' leaders to inspire those under their authority made the Marine Corps a success disproportionate to its size. After all, it was actually the smallest of all the branches of the armed services, yet it had the biggest reputation and the highest morale.

Jeez, now he was sounding like a recruiting commercial.

His inability to sleep was entirely Vanessa's fault. He'd only been with her for one day, and already she'd disrupted his thought processes.

That wasn't all she'd done, either. She'd surprised him, a man who prided himself on never being surprised. And she'd kissed him. How could he have known that she'd turn out to be so...tempting?

A Marine was used to resisting temptation and enforcing self-discipline. He was a "Mustang," an enlisted man who'd worked his way up the ranks to become an officer. He was expected to lead men who considered themselves as tough as nails, so he had to be even tougher. And he was. Normally.

The problem was that nothing about this situation was normal. It wasn't normal for him to have the slightest doubts about the appropriateness of his mission, or to have his loyalty waver in the slightest bit.

Mark sighed again and shoved off the tangled sheet to hit the deck for a series of push-ups. While he was awake he might as well maintain his strength. He had a feeling he was going to need a lot of it to handle this sexy princess.

When Vanessa woke the next morning, she wasn't sure where she was. Then it all came back to her. She was playing hooky with a hunky Marine. Which explained the erotic dreams she'd had last night in the lapping confines of the water bed.

She'd worn her I Love New York T-shirt to bed. Somehow she'd managed to pack only the top to her purple silk pajamas and not the bottoms. She didn't have much experience packing for herself and clearly she didn't have the hang of it yet. Of course, she had been working under extenuating circumstances at the time. Mark had been demanding that she hurry up, and she'd still been recovering from the kiss he'd given her…and she'd returned.

Enough of that. She sat up. She could learn how to pack. She was an intelligent woman. She could do the things normal women did. Like cook.

She'd seen part of a gourmet-cooking show while channel surfing last night. The short segment had shown how to make French toast, and it looked easy enough. She could do that. She *would* do that. Right after taking a shower.

After selecting her clothes, she carefully opened the bedroom door and peeked down the hallway. She could see that Mark was still sleeping on the couch. He didn't look very comfortable. She resisted the temptation to cover his bare chest with the sheet he'd mostly kicked off and instead scurried into the bathroom.

Thank heaven she'd brought along a few basics—soap and a toothbrush. The soap was hand milled in Volzemburg and smelled of carnations. After her shower, she put on a crisp white shirt, paired with her new jeans. They were the new capri length and had a flirty fringe at the hem that moved as she walked. The outfit was fun and represented her newfound freedom.

She was a woman in capri pants, hear her roar. She could do anything. Next up, breakfast.

Mark was still asleep on the couch as she walked into the kitchen and took stock. She didn't question why there were eggs in the fridge already, she just checked the expiration date to make sure they were still good. They were. So was the bread and the milk. Mark must have run out last night and gotten some food after she'd gone to bed.

Good. She had all the ingredients for French toast. It took her a few tries to get the egg-soaked bread from a shallow bowl into the frying pan but she finally managed it. And it took a few tries to get the hang of using the spatula to turn the bread over without mangling it in the process. But she finally did manage.

Syrup. She needed maple syrup. There wasn't any.

"What's going on?" Mark demanded as he joined her in the kitchen.

She was momentarily distracted by his bare chest and legs. He was wearing a pair of military-green boxers and a frown. That was all. His vivid blue eyes were glaring at her as if she was responsible for everything that had ever gone wrong in his life. The Marine was clearly not in a good mood. And he was just as clearly incredibly sexy first thing in the morning, grouchy mood or not.

"What's going on?" she repeated, stalling for time to get her thoughts together. It wouldn't do to be caught drooling over him. "I'm cooking."

"You?" He was clearly skeptical. "Do you know how?"

"Of course I do." She didn't tell him she'd picked up this bit of knowledge from the TV last night. "We need some maple syrup for the French toast."

"Did you look in the kitchen drawer?" he asked.

"No." It seemed a strange place to store a bottle of syrup in her opinion.

"The guy who lent me this place collects those condiment containers from fast-food places." He looked through an assortment of ketchup and mustard packets before saying, "Aha!" He triumphantly held up several small plastic containers of maple syrup. "This stuff probably never saw a maple tree, but it is syrup, and it should taste good on French toast."

"You should get dressed," she briskly told him.

"Yes, ma'am," he drawled.

By the time she'd set out dishes and mugs on the tiny island that served as an eating area, Mark had taken a shower and gotten dressed.

"You did that fast," she noted, impressed by his speed as well as his sexy appearance. His dark hair was still wet.

"The Marine Corps doesn't encourage dawdling."

Her eyes traveled down his body, finally registering what was written on the dark blue T-shirt he wore. When It Absolutely Positively Has To Be Destroyed Overnight—U.S. Marine Corps.

She laughed so hard her sides hurt, and her eyes watered. Not at all a dainty princess laugh.

"I'm sorry," she gasped, trying to regain her dignity.

"Don't be." He smiled at her. "You've got a nice laugh."

Her father had once complained she sounded like a horse neighing when she laughed, not at all appropriate behavior for a royal. So she'd learned to control her laugh as she had every other aspect of her life, to keep it restrained and proper.

"I set the coffee machine on automatic last night, so it should just about be done perking now," Mark was saying.

"That was clever of you."

"That's me. A clever Marine."

"Maybe you should be known as the clever one in your family instead of the proud one," she teased him, and then wondered at the shadow that passed over his face.

The truth was that Mark had gotten teased about being the smart one in his family, a family where strength was valued over all else. None of his brothers were dummies by any stretch of the imagination. But Mark stood out. He'd always wanted to know more. As an officer candidate he'd studied under the blanket with a flashlight at night while the others slept.

He knew about the derogatory comments made by others, often in other branches of the armed forces, about Marines. One frequently used comment was that Marine was an acronym for Muscles Are Required, Intelligence Not Essential. Of course, anyone voicing said opinion was likely to end up on the wrong end of a fistfight.

"Did I say something wrong?" she asked.

His expression hardened as if he regretted letting her see what she had. "No. The French toast isn't half-bad."

"Not half-bad? It's delicious!" she declared, eminently proud of her culinary accomplishment. "The French toast made by the royal chef doesn't taste half this good."

"I wouldn't know." Mark paused for a healthy sip of his black coffee before taking another helping. "I don't eat much food prepared by royal chefs."

"Actually our chef is very good," she said.

"I'm sure he is."

"It's just that *I* made this French toast."

"Yes, you did."

"It's silly, I know, to feel this strong a sense of accomplishment over something as trivial as French toast.''

''Never underestimate the importance of a good breakfast,'' he solemnly told her before digging into his meal.

She watched him eat. What exactly was it about this man that got to her as no other had? Certainly, his blue eyes were gorgeous. The easy-to-look-at lines of his face lent him a reckless attractiveness. And he had a good body. An incredible smile, a sensual mouth, especially his full lower lip. He also had nice hands, she was just noticing that now. Lean, long fingers.

Put all the bits together and you had a man who was like a magnet—pulling at her center, drawing her ever nearer.

He was more than just sexy or attractive. He was powerful. In both the way he carried himself and in everything he did.

Even now, eating breakfast, he still looked as if he could lay down his fork at a moment's notice, grab a machine gun and lead a squad to glory. This man was a warrior at heart.

The warrior and the princess—both accustomed to giving orders and having them obeyed. The resulting interaction was bound to create friction between them.

Vanessa smiled in anticipation. Sometimes friction was a good thing.

''I'm queen of the world!'' Vanessa announced from the front of the ferryboat taking them out to the Statue of Liberty later that morning.

She was rewarded with a faceful of rain as a sudden downpour dropped from the sky as if a heavenly hand had unzipped a pocketful of rain.

''Do you think that was a sign?'' she laughingly

asked Mark as they both hurried to the cover of the cabin.

Mark thought she looked utterly adorable as she stood there, her baseball cap stuck in her pocket so it wouldn't blow off, her sleek hair caught up in two pigtails with a big apple hair fastener he'd bought for her at the souvenir shop back at Battery Park where they'd caught the ferry.

"What's wrong?" she asked. "Do I have something on my face?"

She had happiness written all over her face in big bold letters. What a difference a couple of days made. She'd been so pale when he'd first seen her at her hotel suite, with hollows in her cheeks and dark circles under her eyes. She looked like another woman now. One who'd shed a ton of stress.

He'd seen it before, in the men he commanded. The constant need to be alert, to always keep your guard up took its toll. Combine that with a lack of sleep, and the "fog of war" set in. But that had been in combat conditions. For the first time he was realizing that Vanessa truly had been under a great deal of stress and that her position as a princess had left a mark on her. She'd been a woman at war with herself.

"What is it?" she demanded, almost looking crosseyed in an effort to look at her own chin and nose. She didn't have a mirror with her to check her face. And Mark was looking at her so strangely.

Maybe she should excuse herself and go check a bathroom mirror. Normally her lady-in-waiting packed the contingency items like a makeup bag and mirror in her purse, leaving Vanessa free to worry about other things.

"Nothing," Mark finally replied. "You look fine."

"Do I look like a typical tourist?"

"I don't know that you'll ever look typical," he said with certain wryness.

"I thought I looked very typical," she said, prepared to make her case for normality of appearance.

"You look...cute."

She grinned.

"Come on," he said. "We're about to disembark. Starboard side. Right side," he translated for her.

"How do you know that?"

"The Marine Corps began as a sea service. We use a lot of the same terminology squids do."

"Squids?" she said, confused.

"A Marine's way of referring to Navy personnel."

"Said with affection, no doubt."

"Absolutely," he said with a wicked grin.

"Why, you are just a fountain of information this morning," she said. "Not only do you know your starboard from your left, you also know how to make good coffee."

One dark eyebrow lifted. "A word of advice in the compliment department, it carries more weight if you don't sound so astonished when making the compliment."

"I'll keep that in mind. So you're a diplomatic Marine, hmm?"

"Again, a compliment carries more weight if you don't sound quite so astonished when you're saying it."

"I'm just saying that I'm impressed by your diplomacy. Prudence led me to believe that Marines were a tough-as-nails bunch."

"That we are, ma'am." He cupped his hand under her elbow as he chivalrously assisted her down the plankway.

The sun came out again just as they stepped on land. They walked past the concession building toward a circular area with a flagpole in the center. A profusion of colorful flowers bloomed around the walkway. But it was the sight of the Statue of Liberty directly beyond the American flag that brought an emotional lump to Vanessa's throat. She blinked away an unexpected dampness in her eyes that wasn't caused by the earlier rain.

"You okay?" Mark asked.

She nodded. "My mother was an American citizen. I guess I was just hit with a wave of patriotism for my American heritage. I was actually born in New York City when she returned here for medical reasons. The pregnancy was a difficult one, so my father had her come here."

"How did an American woman end up marrying a king?" Mark had seen the facts in Vanessa's security file, but they didn't tell the story of her life.

"They met at Ascot in England," Vanessa replied. "My mother said it was love at first sight. My father broke with tradition and married outside of European royalty."

"If your father did that, then maybe he's not as strait-laced as you think he is."

"He seems to have forgotten that part of himself," she said quietly. "He's changed since my mother's death. We all have." Vanessa wondered what her mother would have thought about her daughter playing tourist on Liberty Island.

A cloud scuttled over the sun as a group of school-children passed by, jostling Vanessa. Mark gathered her close.

The Statue of Liberty represented the idea of a safe haven for so many millions of people, and here she was, an American-born princess who'd never felt a safer haven than here in her Marine's arms. She closed her eyes and savored the brief moment—the sounds of the soaring seagulls mingling with the steady beat of Mark's heart beneath her ear.

"You okay?"

She could feel as well as hear his husky voice. Why hadn't she noticed the awesome range of his voice before? It could soften to incredible gentleness or harden with powerful authority. It was the kind of voice that brought women to their knees.

"You okay?" he repeated.

She nodded. Much as she might want to, she couldn't just stand here in his arms all day. Reluctantly, she moved away and smiled at him.

His responding roguish grin made her heart perform somersaults.

"Come on, let's go." He held out his hand to her.

She took it, and felt the special connection between them clear to her very soul.

They entered the museum at the base of the statue just as a guide started his spiel.

"The sculptor Frédéric-Auguste Bartholdi had originally envisioned that this statue would mark Egypt's Suez Canal, but history and politics got in the way. He then looked to America."

Vanessa couldn't imagine Lady Liberty being anywhere else but here, welcoming newcomers to America.

"Upon entering, you no doubt noticed the torch," the guide continued. "It is the original torch, which was replaced during the refurbishing of the statue in the 1980s. The statue's iron skeleton was designed by Gustave Eiffel who built a little tower in Paris."

Vanessa smiled. She'd been to the Eiffel Tower several times. But it hadn't had the same effect on her that the Statue of Liberty did. Perhaps because the statue represented what she was looking for—freedom and liberty. The freedom to be herself, to be loved for herself and the liberty to live her own life.

"Where to now?" Mark asked as they departed Battery Park. The view of the Manhattan skyline on the return trip had struck Vanessa with its beauty. So had the view of Mark's face in profile against that skyline. Power and beauty. A potent combination.

She doubted her Marine captain would appreciate her thinking him beautiful. She grinned and linked her arm through his. "Is there any place you'd like to go?" she asked him. "Besides that strip joint you were telling me about," she added with a teasing grin.

"We could make a quick stop at the Met."

"I'd like that."

They stopped at the museum store first, where Mark insisted on buying her a necklace with a miniature silver shoe dangling from it. "Your glass slipper, ma'am."

"But you've already gotten me souvenirs today."

"This is different," he said gruffly. "Just graciously accept it."

She curtsied. "Thank you, kind sir."

"Do you want me to put it on for you?"

"Yes, please." His fingertips brushed against her nape as he struggled with the neck chain's fastener. The chain was short so he didn't have much room to maneuver. Vanessa didn't mind. She just stood there, in the midst of the crowded store, basking in the glow of his meticulous attention as tiny shivers of pleasure chased each other up and down her spine. Her reaction to his touch wasn't diminishing with exposure. If anything, it was increasing.

"There," he finally said. "Let me see how it looks." Placing his hands on her shoulders, he turned her around to face him.

She fingered the necklace, which was a shorter length than her mother's St. Christopher medal, which she wore beneath her top. "How does it look?"

"Perfect."

As she smiled at him, she marked this as a perfect moment in her life. There hadn't been many, so when they did occur, she always took note.

Once inside the museum they held hands as they strolled around the collection of impressionist paintings. Vanessa had seen them once before, on a diplomatic visit when she and her mother had been given a private tour after regular museum hours before going to a special gala ball for the Volzemburg Ballet, something else her country was famous for. She hadn't been back to the Met since then.

"Something wrong?" Mark asked. "You seem awfully quiet all of a sudden."

"I was remembering the last time I was here, when I was fifteen and came with my mother for a private tour. I remember wanting to stay in front of one of Monet's paintings and just soak in the joyful color and light radiating from it. But we couldn't stay because we were on a tight schedule and there was a gala event waiting for us. My mother promised we'd come back again, but she died in a car crash a short while later."

"I'm sorry."

"Thank you." She squeezed his hand in appreciation. "It's just that I still miss her, even after all this time."

"What about the rest of the American branch of your family?" Mark asked, although he already knew the answer from her files.

"My mother was an only child, and her parents died in a plane crash shortly before she did."

"That must have been tough for your family."

"Royalty doesn't show grief, it's not allowed. It's an emotion, and any emotion is to be avoided at all costs."

"Sounds like the Marine Corps."

"Yes, but you *chose* to enlist in the Marines. I had no choice."

Mark wondered if he truly had had a choice. He'd done what was expected of him, and then swerved from tradition by becoming an officer.

Where were these insurgent thoughts coming from? He'd never questioned his place in the Marine Corps before.

It was *her*. Vanessa was questioning her own life choices, which made him question his. Too bad he didn't have any answers.

Chapter Seven

Vanessa had never been so nervous in her life. Not even when she'd met the pope for the first time had she had these kind of butterflies in her stomach.

Actually, butterflies were not really an accurate description—thundering elephants came closer to the truth. And all because she was going out to dinner with Mark.

It shouldn't have been a big deal. She told herself a million times in the past hour that it wasn't a big deal. She had yet to actually *convince* herself of that, however.

The simple black dress she'd bought on sale fit her well. It was a sleeveless cotton sheath that suited her. She'd used one of those fun temporary color shampoos on her hair so no one would recognize her. After all, she couldn't wear her baseball cap out to dinner. It didn't go with her dress.

On the way home this afternoon, she and Mark had stopped at a corner store. While Mark had picked up some more food, she'd picked up the shampoo, a dollar lipstick and a two-dollar eye shadow. Applying her simple makeup, she couldn't help thinking of the royal perfumer who charged thousands of dollars to blend a unique scent just for her. Vanessa hadn't selected the scent, her father had.

She stared at herself in the mirror mounted on the back of the bedroom door. She looked good because she looked happy and carefree. And nervous, yes. But happy.

She'd put a CD in the compact stereo on the bedside table. Judging by the CD collection, Mark's friend had a thing for the Rat Pack singers from the fifties. At the moment Sammy Davis Jr. was singing an old classic about an irresistible force meeting up with an immovable object. Listening to the lyrics, Vanessa decided this one could be a theme song for Mark and her.

Swaying in her bare feet across the hardwood floor, she swirled her way to the corner where she slipped on her new sandals. In addition to her new slipper necklace, she also wore an anklet, a dainty heart with I Love NY etched on it she'd bought at a souvenir store earlier that day. It dangled jauntily, swinging as she danced her way back to the mirror. She felt so decadently... American.

Now Sammy was singing about the best being yet to come. Wouldn't that be wonderful, Vanessa thought. To think the best might be yet to come filled her with a surge of anticipation. The day's freedom had already gone to her head like a fine wine.

She looked over to the snow globe of the NY skyline that Mark had bought for her on Liberty Island. It sat on top of the dresser, where sunlight from the window shimmered off it, reminding her of how much fun she'd had.

"What are you doing in there?" Mark asked from the other side of the door.

"Making myself beautiful," she replied.

"That should take all of about two seconds," he retorted.

Opening the door, she said, "Was that a compliment, Captain?"

He didn't reply. At least not with words. But his blue eyes spoke directly to her heart, stealing her breath away.

When Sinatra started singing "I've Got You Under My Skin," Vanessa knew she was in trouble—not because of Ol' Blue Eyes crooning but because of Mark. He threw her heightened senses into turmoil. A responsive awareness seemed to have taken hold of every muscle and every nerve in her body. And all because Mark was looking at her as if seeing her, really seeing her, for the very first time. He liked what he saw. Male to female. The sensual message was coming across loud and clear.

She liked what she saw. Wearing dark slacks and a dark shirt, he was the epitome of sexy masculinity.

"I like what you did with your hair. You look great," he finally said.

"Thanks, so do you." Her voice was a breathless squeak. Clearing her throat, she added, "I left my tiara behind as you requested."

"Wise move." He nodded approvingly.

"I did consider wearing that green foam crown you got for me at the Statue of Liberty, but I decided it clashed with my outfit."

"We certainly wouldn't want you clashing," he said.

"The little Italian place around the corner has its standards, you know. They might not let us in if you clashed."

"That's what I figured. A place has to have some standards."

"Are you ready?"

She'd asked him that question when they'd left her hotel suite, was it only yesterday morning? She felt as if it had been a lifetime ago. "I'm ready."

"Good." He gallantly offered her his arm. "Shall we go?"

They walked to the restaurant. Strolled, really. It seemed a night made for lovers. Or maybe it was just her, noticing all the couples—the teenagers kissing in a doorway, the elderly couple holding hands at the bus stop.

Her dreamy pleasure continued once they reached Clara's Restaurant. The small eatery had white paper tablecloths instead of damask linens, but she'd never seen a more delightful place. Candlelight flickered from the two dozen or so tables. She and Mark were seated at a tiny table for two in the corner.

"This probably isn't the kind of place you're used to," Mark began.

She interrupted him. "You're talking to a woman who likes pizza and fries, remember?"

He smiled. "Yeah, I remember."

"Then you better guard your dinner plate so I don't steal anything from it."

"You're welcome to try," he invited her with a grin.

The music playing in the background was soft and romantic. Old classics. "Night and Day." "I've Got the World on a String."

It was a little eerie having her evening orchestrated as if her life was a sound track in a movie.

She and Mark talked about their day together, about the things they'd seen and heard. They laughed all through the first course, a delicious homemade minestrone.

They talked about the exhibits they'd seen at the Met. At one point, Vanessa shyly confessed, "I wanted to be an artist. I studied briefly in Paris, but my father needed my help so I returned home and took up my diplomatic duties. I still paint when I can, but it isn't very often. What about you? Have you always wanted to be a Marine?"

"At one time I kicked around the idea of starting my own security firm," he admitted.

"Why didn't you?"

"Because I already have a full-time job as a Marine."

"And that's enough? You haven't ever wondered if there's more to life?"

He'd never used to wonder, but lately he'd started. Since meeting her, his rock-firm Marine world had been turned upside down. Where before he'd always thought he had his life squared away, now doubts were creeping in.

"I don't know," he admitted. He'd never talked this way with anyone before.

She nibbled on the oven-warm bread she'd dipped in olive oil and grated parmesan cheese before saying, "I've definitely got that round-peg-in-a-square-hole feeling. Have had it for years now, in fact. It must be nice to live a life that completes you instead of one that leaves you empty. To be doing something you love, something you believe in with all your heart." She sounded wistful.

"Sometimes you start out loving something, and then things change."

"Or maybe we change?"

"Or maybe it's a bit of both," he said.

She nodded. "I know what you mean."

"You do?" Here he wasn't even sure if what he was articulating was right and yet she seemed to understand.

"Yes, I certainly do. We both have…demanding jobs," she said, aware of the waiter removing their empty dishes and replacing them with their main courses. "And we both work for strong taskmasters who have a very high standard of excellence. But if you have a dream, you should follow it."

"What about you? What about your dream job?"

"It would be working with those children I told you about. I'd love to be able to start a special foundation for them. There are reasons I can't have my dream. As I said, my father has forbidden me from doing more than I already am. What are the reasons you can't have yours?"

"I already told you. I've got a full-time job."

"So you see yourself as what…rising to be a general?"

The music playing now was "Mack the Knife," and it matched the sudden edge to Mark's expression. "There's nothing wrong with being a general."

"I'm sure there isn't."

"It's all about power, about having the power to make sure the Marine Corps gets what it deserves. We're constantly fighting for what's ours because we're the smallest of the armed services."

"So what's your plan? To be the youngest general in Marine history?"

"It's a good goal."

"Yes, it is. Funny how goals are different than dreams, though, isn't it? Your goal is to be the youngest general, but your *dream* is to have your own security business, to be self-employed."

"The Marines aren't big on self or individualism," Mark said. "In their view, the good of many outweighs the good of the few."

"Sounds like the way my father thinks. He's not real big on individualism either. Especially mine."

"˜s your sister as rebellious toward him as you are?"

"My sister is much better at obeying rules than I am or ever could be. She should have been born first so she could be heir to the throne. I'm sure she'd do a better job at it than I ever could."

"I wouldn't say that. You're very good at giving orders."

"Yes, but as you pointed out, I'm not good at taking them. Anna is."

"Your sister's name is Anna?"

"Yes. She looks very much like my mother, petite and dainty, very elegant, always knowing the right thing to say or to wear. Next to her I feel as tall as the Empire State Building. Which reminds me, can we go there tomorrow?"

"You haven't gotten tired of playing tourist?"

"Absolutely not." She slid off her sandal beneath the table and rubbed her foot with her fingers. "My feet are a bit sore though."

"Remind me to give you a foot massage when we get back to the apartment."

She did remind him as soon as they got inside.

Mark turned on the elaborate stereo in the living room and Sinatra started singing "Too Marvelous for Words." Which is exactly how she felt when Mark began massaging her bare foot while she sat on the couch. His touch was too marvelous for words as his fingers moved in a slow sensuous circle over the sole of her foot.

"I have big feet," she said apologetically. "When Prudence and I went to school together as teenagers for that one year, I used to tell her that I had skis for feet, they were so big. Not dainty princess feet at all."

"And I suppose Anna has dainty princess feet."

His comment surprised her. "Yes, she does," Vanessa confirmed. "How did you know that?"

"I know you." He slid a finger between her toes in a move that felt erotically sensual. "Or I'm starting to."

"You certainly know how to make me feel good," she murmured.

He was tempted to say he knew how to make her feel even better, before remembering who she was and why he was there. She was a princess. He was the Marine protecting and deceiving her. It wasn't something he could afford to forget. Ever.

"It's been a long day," he said abruptly, setting her foot back on the couch. "You should get some rest."

And so Vanessa once again left him alone with his laptop computer to fight his inner battles.

The next two days were a repeat of the last two, filled with sightseeing and fun—the Empire State Building, Times Square, Rockefeller Center. And ending with Mark distancing himself from Vanessa, sending her off to bed alone while he completed his e-mail reports to her father.

As his guilt had increased, the length and detail of his reports had decreased. Mark was supposed to recount everything, but he hadn't. He'd focused on the facts and omitted sharing Vanessa's dreams of being an artist or of starting her own charitable foundation to help children or her memories about her mother.

He was betraying her trust. He was following orders. He was trying not to think about it.

Their current surroundings were a good place to forget things. They were in Central Park on a beautiful spring day, surrounded by relatively fresh air and a crowd of people enjoying the sunshine.

"This city's got two baseball teams, five boroughs, one hundred fifty museums and eighteen thousand restaurants," Mark noted, reading from a guidebook. "So where would you like to go to dinner tonight?"

"We haven't even eaten our lunch yet. Where are the fries?" Vanessa asked, peering over his shoulder as he set aside the guidebook to open a large paper bag.

"You wanted a picnic in Central Park. At a picnic you have potato chips," he told her.

"Actually I wanted to stroll around Central Park," she corrected him. "At night. The picnic was your idea."

"An excellent idea," he declared before popping a potato chip in his mouth.

"Are all Marines so modest?" she teased him.

He retaliated by popping a potato chip in her mouth before saying, "Have I ever told you about Chesty Puller?"

"No." Vanessa blinked at his change of subject. "Is she a former girlfriend of yours?" she inquired dryly.

"Chesty is a he not a she. He's a Marine hero."

"Really? It must have been tough growing up with a name like Chesty."

"His full title was Lieutenant General Lewis B. Chesty Puller. He was the only Marine to win the Navy Cross five times for heroism and gallantry in combat. He was an enlisted man and an officer for thirty-seven years. The action that brought him the most acclaim occurred during World War II in the Pacific. His battalion was stretched over a mile-long front and was the only thing between a critical airfield and the enemy. General Puller moved up and down the front line, encouraging his men and directing the defense."

"He sounds like a special hero," she noted softly, sensing that Mark was telling her this story for a reason. She'd suspected that something was bothering him for the past few days, but she couldn't get him to talk about whatever it was.

"Those who served with him say he stalked around under enemy fire as though daring anyone to hit him. He was a born leader who thrived on combat and became a legend to his troops. He's one of the few, the proud. The Marines have plenty to be proud of."

"I'm sure they do." She waited for him to continue, but he fell silent. It was a brooding kind of silence that indicated someone in conflict. She recognized the symptoms because she'd been there herself. At war with herself over how to deal with her life. It wasn't a pleasant place to be.

"Do you want to talk about it?" she asked him.

"Talk about what?" he countered.

"Whatever it is that's been bothering you."

"No." Bang. That quickly he slammed the emotional door in her face. It seemed he'd only let her so close before pushing her away again. She found his behavior frustrating but understandable. He was a Marine, unaccustomed to sharing emotions. She could relate to that.

She couldn't force him to open up to her. She could only be there for him, the way he'd been there for her this past week. And pray that he wasn't regretting sacrificing his vacation time to be with her.

She nervously filled the silence. "Well then, allow me to say that once again you've outdone yourself in selecting the menu for this afternoon's meal. This Reuben sandwich is delicious, but messy," she added with a laugh as she dabbed at her chin for what felt like the tenth time in as many seconds.

"Picnics are supposed to be messy."

"Not where I come from," she murmured, remembering the lawn parties with hundreds of guests dining on the perfectly groomed grounds of the palace in St. Kristoff. Her gown had always been a matter of great discussion, and she'd never seemed to pick the right one.

"You sure you're not getting homesick yet?" Mark asked, no doubt misinterpreting her melancholy expression.

"Are you kidding?" Turning her face skyward to the sun, she murmured, "I may stay here forever."

Mark was saved from having to reply by the sudden appearance of a toddler, a little boy who'd made his way from a nearby picnic blanket to crash their party.

"Hi there," Vanessa greeted him, curving a protective arm around him as he came to her as if he'd known her all his short life. "You're a friendly little fellow, aren't you?"

The little boy grinned up at her.

The impact of Vanessa holding the child hit Mark

with the force of a high-explosive round from a 40mm grenade launcher.

Something deep inside him clicked, as if a lock had tumbled into place opening up a trunkful of trouble. He wanted her. He wanted her holding *his* child.

All his fine talk about his attraction to her being a result of him having gone too long without a woman fell by the wayside. The truth was staring him in the face and yelling at him from his very soul. This was no ordinary attraction, no ordinary woman. This was something powerful and potentially overwhelming.

And because of that it was also something very dangerous, something that had to be kept under lock and key, something that couldn't be acted upon. Never in his life had he been torn between duty and...love? Was that what this was?

"Joshua, where are you?" A frantic woman's voice could be heard over the sound of a nearby radio.

As quickly as he'd appeared, the toddler was scooped up and carried away by his mother. The boy gave a forlorn little wave at Vanessa over his mother's shoulder.

Mark was also waving goodbye to any hope of being able to carry out his orders in a dispassionate manner. He was in a no-win situation here. If he told Vanessa the truth, he'd disobey orders and she'd hate him. If he stopped reporting their activities to her father, he'd be disobeying orders, and she'd be taken from his care and whisked back to Volzemburg. There was no easy way out. There was no way out, period.

Vanessa noticed that Mark was eyeing her strangely. "Something wrong?"

"You like kids."

"Yes, I do. You already knew that. I told you..."

"I know. About wanting to help kids. I just didn't realize..."

"Yes?" she prompted him.

He shook his head. "Never mind."

"Don't you like kids?"

"Yes, I do."

"It's just that I remember you saying that the only thing that scared you was the idea of marriage and being committed to only one woman. I figured that meant you weren't interested in settling down and having kids."

"You said that marriage scared you, too," Mark reminded her.

"For different reasons. It's not that I don't want to get married, but I want to marry for the same reason my mother did. For love."

"And? What's the problem with that?"

Her eyes became shadowed with unhappy memories. "My father has other plans for me," she said tightly. "Can we talk about something else, please? I don't want to think about that now."

"Sure." He'd mastered the art of blocking out thoughts that were too painful to deal with.

Vanessa was pleased with how quickly Mark regained his earlier good mood. She didn't want anything ruining their time together. There was so little time. She didn't want to think about that, either.

She was wearing her flirty capri jeans again today, teaming them this time with a pink knit designer top. Before going to bed last night, she'd washed the temporary red color from her hair. She was once again wearing the Yankees baseball cap and a pair of dollar sunglasses with cherries on the sides.

Her father would have a fit if he saw her now. She grinned.

"What are you smiling about now?" he asked.

"A woman has to have a few secrets." Leaning forward, she startled him by quickly kissing him. His lips were warm against hers as she brushed against them in a seductive caress that was there and then gone, much as she was tempted to linger.

"What was that for?" His voice was low and rough with suppressed emotions.

"The Reuben sandwich," she said demurely.

Mark tried to keep his wits about him, but she was making it hard. She was definitely making certain parts of his anatomy hard. She looked so delectable sitting there in the sunshine, a happy tourist in a sea of people out enjoying the beautiful spring weather.

But appearances could be deceiving. The two guys playing a game of Frisbee kept getting closer and closer with each toss. Harmless high jinks? Or was it something else? Kidnapping was big business these days. He'd been in Washington long enough to know all about security measures that public figures had to take for their own safety.

He couldn't afford to let Vanessa distract him with her sudden kamikaze kisses. He had a job to do here. The Frisbee-tossers were definitely getting too close for his comfort level. He glared at the men, who quickly moved away. Far, far away.

But that left the man and woman taking pictures of people in the park. What was that about? They must have taken an entire roll of film. Leaning closer to Vanessa, he said, "Don't make any sudden moves, but I want you to casually look to your right. See those people with the camera? Do you recognize them? Paparazzi maybe?"

He had to give her credit, she did just as he asked,

casually turning her head in a way that wouldn't tip anyone off that anything might be amiss.

"I don't recognize them, but there are so many paparazzi. Do you think they're taking pictures of us?"

"I don't know. But I don't like it."

She didn't like it either. She didn't want her royal reality intruding on her perfect day. "Should we leave?"

"Affirmative." It was the first time today she'd heard him sound like a military man.

Mark used his training to make sure that anyone trying to follow them wouldn't have an easy time of it. He took a circuitous route out of the park, hailed a cab and took it to a huge department store.

"You're taking me shopping?" Vanessa said. "I can't believe it."

"Don't believe it." His voice was curt. "We won't be here long." He rushed her out an exit on a different street where he hustled her into another cab before she could catch her breath. He got in so quickly after her that he almost landed on her lap.

Mark gave that driver another address. They ended up taking two more cab rides before finally going to the brownstone. Throughout it all, Mark refused to tell her anything.

Vanessa put up with that until they walked into the apartment. Then she wanted some answers. "Do you want to tell me what that was all about?"

"I was just being cautious."

She knew he wasn't telling her the entire story. Something had been bothering him all afternoon. She wanted to know what it was. "You were cautious by spending a small fortune on cab fares?"

"I didn't like the look of that couple taking pictures at the park."

She hated it when he avoided telling her the whole story, when he got all closemouthed this way, saying as little as possible in short military sentences. "Which would explain why we left the park, not why we had to take three or four cabs to get home."

"Confuse the enemy."

"You think someone was following us?"

"I didn't want to take any chances."

"You don't like taking chances?"

"Not where your safety is concerned."

"I appreciate that. What about the rest of your life?" she surprised him by asking. "Do you take chances there?"

"I'm a Marine. I've dealt with dangerous situations before. Risk is always a factor."

"I was talking about your private life. Do you take chances there? Do you ever do something on the spur of the moment?" She knew he'd used his vacation time to come see her in New York, which hadn't been planned, but he'd already told her he'd only done that because Prudence had asked him. It hadn't been an impetuous move on his own.

"The Marine Corps doesn't like spur-of-the-moment life-styles." His voice was clipped. "We work with discipline, rules and regulations."

"And you like working within the rules? Always coloring between the lines? At the restaurant the other night I asked you if you never wondered if there wasn't something more to life."

"And I said I didn't know."

"A cautious answer if ever I heard one," she scoffed.

"I'm a cautious kind of guy," he stubbornly maintained.

"I find that hard to believe."

They stood, almost nose to nose, like two combatants in a war of wills.

The tense moment was interrupted by the sound of his cell phone ringing.

"It's Prudence for you," Mark said, handing the phone over.

As Vanessa sailed off into the bedroom in a royal huff, Mark realized how close he'd come to losing his objectivity today. Who was he kidding? He *had* lost his objectivity. And there was no getting it back. Which meant he'd have to deal with it and get on with his mission.

Mark knew all about the nature of war—the friction, the uncertainty, the fluidity. The nature of sex held many similarities. But he knew diddly-squat about the nature of love.

He'd always had a plan for his life. He wouldn't fall in love and marry until he was thirty-five. That way he'd be mature enough not to make a mistake like his brother Justice had when he'd married so young. Mark had seen how devastated the divorce had left his brother, and he didn't aim on making the same mistakes. Sure, his younger brother Joe was married already, but Joe was much more impetuous than Mark was.

No, Mark preferred a logical game plan to the blindly following-your-heart school of thought. Give him a clearly defined objective, and he'd design a campaign that would achieve and secure that objective.

Marine Corps doctrine demanded that officers be men

of action and of intellect both. Mark had to be resolute and self-reliant in his decision-making.

Whatever had hit him when he'd seen Vanessa holding that child at the park, he had to get over it. He had to get real here. What could a Marine like him offer a princess like her? Not much.

He couldn't be swayed, couldn't let himself be distracted, couldn't let his loyalty be divided. To do so could prove disastrous—not only for him but for Vanessa as well.

Chapter Eight

"Mark is driving me crazy," Vanessa told Prudence over the phone as she flung herself onto the bed before remembering it would ripple and bob.

"You're not falling for him, are you?" Prudence asked.

Sexy Marines and water beds weren't made for falling. Picturing one particular sexy Marine on this water bed temporarily rendered her speechless.

Prudence filled in the silence. "Because when Joe and I were marooned together in that cabin in a snowstorm, he drove me crazy, too."

Vanessa looked outside, catching sight of the snow globe Mark had given her as she did so. "There's no snowstorm here." She got up and retrieved the snow globe, turning it upside down to watch the white flakes swirl. "Sunny skies all the way." But inside, Vanessa felt as if a storm was indeed raging, sparked by Mark's way of getting closer to her only to end up pushing her away. She'd tried to be understanding at first, but her patience was running out.

"The sun may be shining there, but Mark is one of the sexy Wilder brothers." Prudence did not sound convinced. "I know firsthand how potent their sex appeal can be."

"Oh, please," Vanessa scoffed. "I'm a princess. I've met the sexiest men in the world."

"And never been as rattled by one of them as you are right now by Mark."

"That's because he's…" she sputtered. She actually sputtered. Unsettled by her reaction, she placed the snow globe he'd given her back on the dresser as if it were responsible for her sudden incoherence.

"At a loss for words?" Prudence teased her. "A sure symptom of imminent attraction."

"The man kissed me the first day I met him and then had the nerve to say it was my fault. That I shouldn't have let him kiss me." The words were tumbling from her now. "Then ten minutes later, he kisses me again, supposedly to distract Anton, but who knows? Today I kissed Mark, and he just gave me this look."

"You do realize you're not making any sense, don't you?" Prudence noted.

"I know," Vanessa replied forlornly, returning to sit on the bed.

"Did you like Mark's kisses?" Prudence bluntly asked.

"Too much," Vanessa candidly replied.

"Yes, well, Mark is the complicated one in the family."

"I thought he was the proud one. The smart one."

"He's both those things, which makes him complicated. Mark goes through life with a battle plan laid out in his mind. And he's enough of a Marine not to tell anyone what that battle plan is. But I don't think it involves things like falling in love. I suspect he doesn't want to lose control of a situation enough to have his emotions take over.''

''Why not? What's so bad about emotions?''

''We're talking about a Marine here,'' Prudence reminded her. ''Mark was raised in a family of Marines. So was I. Trust me, emotions are *not* something Marines are proud of. If they could ban them in their procedural handbook, I'm sure they would.''

Vanessa sighed. ''My father has the same mind-set. Emotions are not allowed in a royal family, either.''

''Which is one of the reasons you and I are such good friends,'' Prudence said. ''We both grew up in stiff-upper-lip environments, and we both rebelled against that regimented life-style.''

''You swore you'd never get involved with a military man.''

Prudence laughed. ''Yes, well, now you know first-hand how tempting they can be.''

''Is that why you sent Mark here?'' Vanessa countered. ''To show me how tempting he can be?''

''Hey, if you married him, we'd be sisters-in-law.''

''The only problem with that is Mark, who probably has his own grand pooh-bah plan for marriage that doesn't include getting hooked up with a princess. And then there's my father, who has plans of his own for me.''

''One of the tabloids is saying that you and Sebastian are on the verge of announcing your engagement,'' Prudence said.

Vanessa closed her eyes and groaned. She had no doubt who had leaked that story. The royal press officer

Oscar Mullion was one of her father's most devoted minions. And one of her sternest critics.

"They clearly think they can coerce me into marrying Sebastian," Vanessa muttered angrily, "but it won't work."

"Have you talked to your father lately?"

"Not since I took off, no."

"Aren't you supposed to check in with him?"

"Yes, I am." Vanessa checked her watch, a simple solid gold design from a top Swiss designer. Mark had let her keep her watch, saying that so many cheap knockoffs were sold on the streets of New York that no one would know this one was real. "It's too late now, I'll have to do that first thing in the morning. With the time change, it's already the middle of the night there."

"Then let's get back to the subject of Mark," Prudence said eagerly.

"He's doing this one-step-forward-two-steps-back ritual mating dance with me," Vanessa griped. "Stop laughing!"

"I can't help it," Prudence gasped. "I'm just picturing Mark in dress blues doing any kind of ritual mating dance."

"It was just a phrase. And he's not wearing any uniform here. Just jeans and a T-shirt, if that much."

"Oh-ho, so that means you've seen him in less than jeans and a T-shirt." Prudence's voice was filled with glee. "You've been holding back on me. Tell me more."

"He sleeps on the couch in the living room here at his friend's apartment where we're staying. And naturally he can't sleep in his jeans."

"Naturally not. So exactly how much of Mark have you seen?"

"Stop that!" Vanessa scolded her with a laugh. "He's wearing perfectly respectable military-green boxers to sleep in at night."

"Perfectly respectable, huh?" Prudence's voice was wickedly naughty.

"Don't distract me, I was trying to ask you a question earlier. Getting back to my one-step-forward analogy, is that how Mark is with other women?"

"I don't think so. He tends not to get very serious about any one of them. I heard him telling Joe once that he had a plan, and that marriage didn't fit into that plan until he was thirty-five."

"How nice to have your life so clearly mapped out like that," Vanessa said tartly.

"Your life is practically mapped out until you're thirty-five," Prudence pointed out.

"And I hate it."

"So what are you going to do about it?"

"Well, I can tell you one thing," Vanessa replied. "I am definitely not marrying Sebastian, whatever those tabloids say."

"The princess cannot be disturbed right now," Celeste firmly told Anton early the next morning. "As you can see, she has not finished her breakfast yet." She indicated the tray, where a soft-boiled egg was half eaten, the spoon still in the shell. "She is taking a shower. You can hear the water running in the bathroom."

Anton nodded, but said, "I have not seen her in almost a week."

"Because she is ill. You know that. The doctor has been here—"

"I do not trust him," Anton interrupted her to state. "I have seen the way he makes eyes at you."

"Dr. Rosenthal has been very kind."

"He has ties to the U.S. military. I checked him out."

Celeste glared at Anton. "The princess will be furious with you. You had no right to do that. She chose this doctor personally."

Anton did not back down. "The princess should be seeing the royal physician."

"He's back in Volzemburg."

"He could fly in to see her."

"She's not that ill that he has to do that."

Anton frowned at her. "Something is very suspicious here. I do not like this at all."

"It is not your job to pass judgment on what the princess does or the choices she makes."

"I am here to protect her."

"Then do that, and do not make her illness even more difficult by making trouble."

"Is there a problem here?" Dr. Rosenthal asked from the open doorway into the suite.

"No. Anton was just expressing his concern about the princess. I told him that while she is feeling a bit better, she cannot be disturbed by him at the moment."

"She is well enough to see the doctor," Anton said.

"If she was all that well, I wouldn't need to see her," Dr. Rosenthal pointed out.

"Tell Her Highness that I wish to speak with her at her earliest convenience," Anton said forcefully.

Celeste replied, "I will tell her."

Anton angrily returned to his post outside the suite, but not before giving Dr. Rosenthal a hard-edged disapproving look.

"Are you all right?" Dr. Rosenthal asked Celeste.

"You have been very kind these past few days, Dr. Rosenthal. I don't know what I would have done without your support."

"Please, call me Abraham." He smiled at her. "I've been glad to be of assistance, Celeste. I've come to look forward to our visits."

She blushed. "I have as well…Abraham."

"When I speak with Mark later today I will tell him that Anton is putting pressure on you." His kind gaze was filled with empathy, and Celeste was caught up in the moment.

The phone rang, interrupting them. "Celeste, this is Princess Vanessa calling. How is everything?"

Celeste quickly filled her in about Anton's increasing suspicion. She closed by saying, "I fear the king will be calling next and demanding to speak with you, Your Highness."

"I'm surprised he hasn't done so yet. But not to worry, I'm going to call him now. I just wanted to check in with you first to make sure everything was all right, that you were managing things at your end."

"I have been managing with Abraham's assistance. He has been most helpful," Celeste said.

"Abraham?"

"Dr. Rosenthal."

"Ah. It sounds like the two of you have been hitting it off."

Celeste blushed again. "Yes, Your Highness."

"Give…Abraham my thanks for his assistance."

"I will, Your Highness."

"And Celeste…"

"Yes, Your Highness?"

"I'm glad you've got someone helping you. I think

the two of you would make a lovely couple. I'll be in touch again tomorrow.''

Celeste was too flustered to even say goodbye.

''Your Majesty, Her Royal Highness Princess Vanessa is on the phone,'' Oscar Mullion said.

''I'll speak with her.'' With an imperious wave of his hand, King Leopold of Volzemburg took the phone from his press officer. ''You should have called sooner, Vanessa.''

She tried not to be disappointed that his very first words were already filled with disapproval. She also had to remember to keep her voice husky and low, as if she were getting over laryngitis. ''I'm sorry, Father.''

''Have you been enjoying your…rest?''

''The rest has done me good, I believe,'' she carefully replied.

''When will you be returning home to the palace?'' King Leopold demanded.

''The doctor said I could not fly for a week.''

''That was almost five days ago.''

''He has not changed his mind.''

''We need you back here, Vanessa. Sebastian has been most concerned.''

''Tell him thank you, but there is no need for him to be worried.''

''As your fiancé, naturally your health is a matter of concern for him.''

''He is not my fiancé!'' Vanessa almost forgot to keep her voice low. ''He is not my fiancé,'' she repeated more quietly this time. ''I wish you would stop saying that he is.''

''Your stubbornness is not an appealing trait, Vanessa.''

It hurt to hear him tell her that, even though she knew that her father found little about her appealing. "I must go, Father. The cell-phone battery is flashing."

"Remember, Vanessa, you have responsibilities."

"Goodbye, Father."

King Leopold handed the phone back to his press officer and said, "The e-mail reports I have been getting are becoming briefer and briefer."

Oscar replied, "I agree that is cause for concern, Your Majesty. Then there is this photograph that I just received from my contacts in New York."

King Leopold looked at the picture of his daughter in Central Park. His face darkened ominously. "You know what must be done."

Oscar nodded. "Yes, Your Majesty. And I will see that it is done properly."

"I did not leave one prison just to enter another one," Vanessa angrily informed Mark later that afternoon. "You've kept me locked up here all day!"

"It's pouring rain outside."

"I'm not made out of sugar," she retorted. "I won't melt."

Maybe not, but *he* was about to melt. Vanessa certainly made him hot enough. She was wearing that blue dress with the little flowers on it that she'd gotten at the department store. It showed off her great legs. And the scooped neckline showed off her bare skin and a sexy hint of cleavage. She wasn't wearing her slipper necklace today. Instead, the gold necklace with a St. Christopher medallion rested in the hollow of her throat, tempting him to travel there and taste her with his kisses, with his tongue.

"Listen, Princess, being locked up in such close confines with you hasn't been any piece of cake for me either," he said tightly.

His words infuriated and hurt her. She'd already been feeling vulnerable after her brief conversation with her father, she certainly didn't need Mark adding salt to her wounds. He'd been acting like a bear ever since they'd left the park yesterday afternoon.

"What is wrong with you?" she demanded.

"Nothing is wrong with me."

"Then why have you been acting so grouchy all day?"

"What do you want from me?" Mark angrily demanded.

"What do you want to give me?" she retorted.

Awareness vibrated the very air between them as they stood face-to-face. He was glaring at her with male irritation, mixed with a very healthy dose of sexual awareness. His expression was wild, fierce and hot—which was exactly how she felt. Her breath caught at the blatant desire that flared in his gaze.

"What do I want to give you? A lecture," he growled. "Don't you have a practical bone in your body?"

"Why don't you check for yourself?" she retorted, holding her arms out, daring him to touch her.

His flame-blue eyes scorched their way down her body even as he growled, "Don't tempt me."

"Why not? I thought Marines were so self-disciplined that they're immune to temptation."

"Believe me, Princess, I am not immune." His voice was strained.

Mark took three steps back, putting the couch between them. It was either that or tumble them both to the floor and make wild love to her until she moaned her surrender and her pleasure. He had to keep a lid on his feelings, on his body. She had no idea what she was asking of him, had no idea what his giving in to her would mean. He had to be the responsible one here.

"Okay, to keep you happy, we'll go out to dinner," he stated in his best officer voice, the one filled with authority.

Unfortunately it appeared to have no effect on Vanessa. "We're going out all right. To dinner and then a dance club afterward. There's one written up in the newspaper that sounds very intriguing."

"We are not going to a dance club."

"Fine. I'll go. You can stay here and keep brooding like you've been doing all day long."

"Don't you get it? I'm responsible for you."

His words hurt her yet again. He was making it clear to her that he was only with her out of a sense of duty to his family, because Prudence had asked for his help. But if that was the case, then why had he looked at her as he had, the way a lean and hungry tomcat eyes a saucer of cream?

It didn't make sense. Unless he was fighting his feelings for her? Was that why he kissed her and then pushed her away? Why he stared at her a few minutes ago as if he'd pay a king's ransom to kiss her again?

"I'm going out to get some fresh air," he muttered. "I'll be back in ten minutes." He slammed out of the apartment.

Why did he have to be so…complicated?

Here he was the first man to ever treat her like a woman instead of a princess. The first man who made her want him with every fiber of her being.

She'd always longed to be loved for herself, for the woman beneath the tiara. It had never happened. So she'd kept striving, kept trying to please everyone so they'd love her. And ended up almost hating herself.

Mark wasn't like men in the European aristocracy or the American blue bloods who had escorted her over the years. He wasn't like Sebastian. He was…Mark. Complicated, sexy, infuriating, sexy, funny, honest, direct, sexy. He saw her for who she was, and while she aggravated him at times and even angered him on occasion, she didn't disappoint him. He'd never demeaned her opinions, even when he disagreed with them. Sure, he'd said a walk in Central Park at night was a dumb idea, but he hadn't made her feel dumb for suggesting it.

He didn't kowtow to her, he didn't patronize her.

He didn't kiss her. Why not? She was pretty certain he wanted to. She definitely knew *she* wanted him to.

Maybe tonight would be the night.

In the end, Mark did accompany her to the dance club. It was either that or lock her in the bedroom. Once he saw her outfit, he certainly had second thoughts about not doing that. And locking himself in there with her.

She was wearing hot-pink, skintight pants in some sort of shiny material and a paler pink shimmery tube top that left her midriff and shoulders bare.

"Where did you get those clothes?" he practically croaked.

"In Paris, why?"

"How did they get here?"

"I packed them in your duffel bag."

"You wear clothes like that as a princess?"

"I'm off duty tonight," she replied. "My dresser didn't know I brought this along. But I was coming to

New York, and I wanted to bring something special just in case I got up the nerve to make a break for it.''

She'd put on her eye makeup with a heavier hand tonight, accentuating her exotically tilted green eyes. She'd also used a luscious, glossy hot-pink lipstick that made a man weak at the knees. She'd used the temporary red hair color shampoo again, only this time she'd done something to her hair to make it stick out in sexy disarray.

She looked like a wild woman intent on seducing a man, not like a prim-and-proper princess.

"Are you sure you want to wear that outfit?" he began.

She interrupted him to firmly state, "I'm positive. And don't even think about trying to put your sweatshirt with the hood on me tonight." Her glare held a regal warning.

"I wouldn't dream of it. But what about a raincoat?" He dived into the closet and retrieved a long trench coat.

"The rain has stopped, and I'd drown in that. It's miles too big for me."

"You'll get cold."

"Not to worry." She patted his arm. "I have a big strong Marine to keep me warm."

Various ways in which he could keep her warm, all of which involved removing his or her clothing or both, immediately filled his mind with X-rated images.

Vanessa knew she was getting to him. She could tell by the glazed look in his blue eyes, by the hunger in his gaze.

He watched her like a hawk throughout their dinner in a trendy Thai bistro with avant-garde furnishings. Afterward they headed for the Meatpacking District and the latest hot spot Vanessa had read about.

They were stopped by the bouncer at the door. "Sorry," the burly man said with a nod at Mark, who was wearing his customary dark jeans with a dark blue shirt. "We're full up."

"Excuse me?" Vanessa blinked, unable to believe she was being turned away. Nothing like that had ever happened to her before. No one turned away Princess Vanessa Von Volzemburg. Of course, she wasn't here as a princess.

"Too bad," Mark said cheerfully. "We'll just head on home then…"

"Absolutely not," Vanessa said. "There are a number of other hot spots in this area. We'll just walk until we find one."

She took off without him, making Mark rush after her. "Hold on a second."

"Look." She pointed to a place on across the street and down a block. "That place looks promising."

Mark had doubts about a bar called Trouble, but Vanessa was hell-bent on going there. This time the bouncer waved them through. Mark quickly checked the place out, noted exits, possible threats, the layout of the floor plan. Not an easy thing to do given the dim light in the bar. A sign by the front door had announced the hip-hop fusion party going on tonight. He'd paid their cover and began to lead Vanessa to a table in a corner, where their backs would be to the wall and where he could see people entering.

The place was beyond crowded, it was jam-packed. The people on the tiny dance floor weren't so much dancing as they were swaying in place to the loud music. It took them forever to get to the corner table he'd eyed, and by the time they arrived there, someone else had already taken it. Vanessa snagged a nearby table and tugged him down beside her.

The drinks were flowing too easily, which made Mark uneasy. He'd been in enough bars in his life as a Marine to know that drunken rowdy crowds were volatile things. There weren't enough servers to take drink orders fast enough, which was further upping the tension in the packed room.

When trouble came, it came fast. An angry shove, a shouted curse, and a fight broke out. Mark reached across the table only to have it collapse beneath the weight of a guy who was sent flying from the table to their right. Half a dozen or more people were now involved in the fight as Mark dodged a fist while desperately searching for Vanessa. She'd simply disappeared!

Chapter Nine

Vanessa had never felt such terror. One minute everything had been going fine. She'd been studying the drinks menu and trying to decide if she wanted a French martini or an apple martini. Then all hell had broken out. She'd looked up to see Mark reaching for her an instant before a man crashed onto their table.

She'd leaped to her feet to avoid being crushed by the falling table. Another man leaped on top of the fallen man, and more jumped on top of him as the fight continued. All the people around her were shoving, women were screaming, she was hemmed in. The incident with the wild shoppers at the department store paled in comparison to this. There was real danger here. Real violence. Exploding all around her. Fists flying, men grunting and cursing.

Where was Mark? Was he okay? Or had he been hurt when that man had fallen into their table?

Vanessa didn't know what to do. She couldn't move, there was no way through the mob. Was that the flash of a knife to her right? She ducked and frantically searched for Mark.

Fear left a metallic taste in her mouth, and she was shaking. Where was Mark? She had to find him. She couldn't panic. She had to think clearly.

But she couldn't. She had no experience with this kind of situation. Chairs were being tossed around and smashed, so were glasses and bottles. Someone grabbed her from behind, and she did what Mark had taught her, she stomped on her attacker's foot. In case her sandals didn't do the job, she also performed a backward kick to the groin. Her attacker grunted and released her.

She whirled away, only to be grabbed again. She was about to repeat her self-defense moves when she looked over her shoulder and realized Mark was holding her. She almost fainted with relief.

But there was no time for that.

"Come on!" he shouted over the bedlam, leading her toward an emergency exit behind the stage area near them. She felt the cool air a second before they reached the open door, following a stream of people trying to get out of harm's way.

When Vanessa's sandal came undone and fell off, she kept going, hopping to keep up with Mark. Once they were in the alley and he realized her predicament, he swept her up in his arms and kept going. Curling her arms around his neck, she rested her head on his shoulder.

She loved this man. The realization was flashing across her mind like one of those huge neon signs in Times Square. She *loved* him.

The doubts, the uncertainties were washed away. Her emotions had been distilled by the trauma she'd just been through, condensed to their purest and rawest form. She loved him. It didn't matter that she was a princess and he was a Marine. That she had responsibilities in her own country and he had a duty to his.

The only thing that mattered was Mark.

She kissed his jaw, so relieved that he hadn't been hurt. He responded by tightening his hold on her. "Hang on, honey."

Honey, not princess. It was the first endearment he'd ever spoken to her.

Her heart swelled.

He turned right out of the alley and headed for the street corner. There he set her on her feet only long enough to whistle like a pro for a cabbie. One instantly obeyed his command and swerved across two lanes of traffic to get to them.

Once they were safely ensconced in the back of the cab, Mark wrapped her in his arms.

"I was so afraid you were hurt," she whispered, reaching up to cup his cheek with her trembling hand.

He pressed a kiss into her palm. "Me? What about you? Are you okay? Did anyone hurt you? Did you sprain your ankle when your sandal broke?"

"I'm fine. Oh, Mark..." Her voice cracked.

"Shh." He gazed down at her with blue eyes that had gone dark with emotion. Tipping her chin up, he lowered his head to brush his lips against each corner of her mouth before settling on the sweet fullness in between. The featherlight caress was all the more commanding because of its possessive gentleness.

This man may have just saved her life. Not just by rescuing her from the fight that had broken out in that bar, but by kissing her. Only now was she realizing how much she'd longed for this, how starved she was for his touch.

The power of her love for him shook Vanessa to her soul. He wasn't kissing a princess, he was kissing *her*. She responded the way any woman in love would, by parting her lips and inviting him in. He sipped delicately at her mouth, as if afraid to frighten her with the full force of his passion.

She'd never seen this side of him, this tender, protective side. Yet she sensed the energy coiled inside him, the power.

He cradled her close, drawing her across his lap so that she was draped over his thighs. He handled her with such sweet finesse that she thought she'd die from the excitement burning within her.

Who knew what tomorrow would bring? The danger tonight had brought home to her that their time together was infinitely precious and had to be celebrated. No more waiting, no more uncertainty. She undid the top buttons of his shirt so that she could place her hands on his bare chest.

Softly crooning in her ear, Mark encouraged her actions, setting her on fire as he traced her bare earlobe with his moist tongue. She was glad she wasn't wearing any earrings because she didn't want anything getting in between his tongue and her skin. The same held true for his hands. He slid them from her bare midriff beneath her soft tube top to caress her even softer bare breasts.

"I wondered all night what you were wearing beneath this top," he murmured as he placed a string of openmouthed kisses from her ear to the hollow of her throat where the slipper necklace he'd given her rested.

"Now you know," she whispered, tightening her arms around his neck.

Taking her face between his hands, he kissed her

without restraint, devouring her with a fierce hunger. Vanessa was lost in a firestorm of accelerating and exhilarating pleasure. The wildness she'd sensed in their very first kiss was still there, as was her delight in the tantalizing moves of his tongue. Heat radiated from his body to hers and from hers to his. She was both powerless and powerful, both the seducee and the seducer.

Unlike that first time, now she knew that she and Mark shared something awesome. She knew the power of her own emotions for him, and she gloried in that knowledge, sharing her passion with him as best she could in the speeding cab.

Their kiss took on a new urgency that was interrupted a few moments later by the sound of the cab screeching to a halt and the cabbie clearing his throat. "We are here," he announced with an Indian accent.

Mark broke off the kiss, leaning his forehead against hers. Vanessa could feel his pounding heartbeat beneath her fingertips. "Yes, we are here." And the way he said it made her think that *here* was a pretty awesome place to be. *Here* was a turning point in their relationship, the point of no return. She couldn't wait.

Apparently neither could Mark because the instant he paid the cabbie he swept her back into his arms and whisked her up the stairs.

"I can walk," she told him in between fierce kisses.

"I know." Mark paused at every landing to show her why staying in his arms was a better idea. And he took his time doing it.

He couldn't get enough of her. Kissing her just made him want her more. Every second brought new discoveries. That she moaned when he teased the roof of her mouth with his tongue. That she shivered when he nibbled on her lower lip. That he went up in flames when she did the same to him.

He slowly slid her to the tiled floor outside the apartment's front door, letting her body brush against his. Her sweet scent drove him mad. Carnations. He'd been smelling carnations for days. And nights. How he'd fantasized about her during the long and sleepless nights.

But even his hottest fantasies weren't as incredible as the reality of being able to curve his hands around her lush derriere and pull her close to his throbbing arousal. She smiled in the dim light of the hallway and rubbed against him with primal feminine enticement.

Growling, he pinned her to the wall, lifting her leg so that she wrapped it around his hips. She braced her bare foot against the back of his thigh as she pressed closer. His hands shifted up and around to once again slide beneath the temptation of her tube top. He brushed his thumbs against her taut nipples and watched her face flush with passion.

"I've wanted to do this from the first moment I saw you in that purple robe of yours." His voice was soft and rough with desire. He lifted the tube top just enough out of his way on one side so that he could bathe her breast with kisses.

Sighing, she slid her fingers through his dark hair and held him closer, her nails raking his scalp.

When he finally took her bare breast into his mouth, she arched her back with unspoken bliss. He caressed her nipples with a tongue made warm and wet from her kisses.

Vanessa thought she'd go up in flames right there, right then. She was filled with a taut urgency that was spiraling out of control. Her lower body was pressed tightly against his and still it wasn't close enough.

She loved the way he was making her feel. She loved him.

She couldn't wait to show him how much.

He made her feel more like a woman than she'd ever felt before. He'd never seemed impressed that she was a princess. But right now he was huskily murmuring his awe and approval of her body and the way she made his respond.

"Feel what you do to me," he groaned, moving against her, his hips surging against hers.

"I want to feel even more," she whispered. "Let's go inside."

"Are you sure?"

"We've wasted enough time." She undid the final button on his shirt and tugged it from the waistband of his pants. "I want us to be together," she murmured against his bare chest, licking the saltiness from his skin. "Where's the key?"

"Key?" he repeated in a dazed voice.

"To the apartment." She slid her hand into his right trouser pocket only to be surprised at what she found there. "Oh my!" She hesitantly stroked him through the material. "Oh my!"

Mark dug into his other pocket and thrust the key into the lock even as he thrust his tongue into her mouth for a searing kiss that spoke of a raw passion running out of control.

Without lifting his lips from hers, he backed her into the darkened apartment, not bothering to turn on the lights as he aimed her for the couch. He'd be lucky if he could make it that far. He wanted to take her right here, right now, right where they stood.

Danger! His warrior's instinct gave him the dire

warning a split second before the lights were suddenly switched on.

He immediately thrust her behind him as he faced the intruders.

He could feel her shifting against his back as she readjusted her tube top before peering around his shoulder. "Oscar! How dare you!" Her voice was filled with regal outrage.

Mark's gut clenched.

Vanessa grabbed his hand as if to tug him out the door with her, as if she was planning on making a run for it with him by her side.

Oscar was not alone. He'd brought three royal security guards with him. Mark recognized one of them as the guy with the camera in Central Park.

"Captain Wilder, the king is most dissatisfied with your most recent reports," Oscar declared. "We feel you have not been entirely forthcoming with us."

The words halted Vanessa in her tracks. Her father's press officer was speaking to Mark as if he knew him.

Her heart began a slow pound of dread. "Reports?" she repeated. "What reports?" Turning to face Mark, she said, "What reports?"

The guilty look in his eyes made her heart stop. When it began beating again, she was a different woman. A woman betrayed.

"No." Her voice was wobbly with emotion. Shaking her head, she dropped his hand as if it were poisoned. "No."

The pain was overwhelming. She couldn't speak, couldn't think. She could only gaze at the man she loved with mute despair.

"Vanessa, listen to me. You don't understand. This wasn't my idea. I was ordered to report to your father."

Mark reached out to her, but Vanessa pushed him and his words away.

She fell back on her years of training, of hiding her feelings, of playing the role of a princess completely unaffected by human emotions. Hard as it was, she regained control. She had to. It was either that or fall into a million tiny pieces right where she stood.

"Oh, I understand perfectly." Her voice was now icy cold. The transformation was complete, from woman in love to ice princess.

"No, you don't," Mark began, only to be interrupted by her father's minion.

"If Her Highness says she understands, then I'm sure she does understand," Oscar said with a prissy smirk that Mark wanted to wipe off his face. The small man had dark beady eyes and a thin mustache. He also had the pompous manner of someone capable of misusing power. "What I don't understand is how you could allow her to go out in such attire."

"You go too far, Oscar," Vanessa warned him in a steely voice.

Oscar bowed his head with false remorse. "I apologize if I have offended you, Your Highness, but I fear the king will be even further offended by your... clothing."

"So he hired a U.S. Marine to act as my nanny? He must have had to pull a number of strings to do that."

Turning to face Mark, she said, "Just tell me one thing. Did Prudence know about this?"

"No," Mark assured her, hurriedly rebuttoning his shirt and stuffing it back into his pants. "Prudence had no part in any of this."

Vanessa had to look away. She was the one who'd wantonly undone his shirt, who'd kissed and caressed him like a besotted fool. She was ashamed in a way that hurt and made her feel ill.

"Your father bugged your phone at the Plaza Hotel," Mark said. "And when you called Prudence and talked about your plan, he knew about it. I'd already agreed to come help you when your father contacted the State Department and through them, the Marines."

"I don't believe you." She'd deal with her father later. What she didn't believe was that Mark had already agreed to come to New York. He'd been ordered to do that, ordered to spy on her.

"Your Highness, the king feels you've spent enough time in New York," Oscar pompously stated, bending his head to her with feigned obsequiousness. "He feels that it's time you return to your duties in our homeland. We shall have to have the royal hairdresser do something with you before the king sees you."

"The hair color is temporary." Now Vanessa was the one who bent her head, as if unable to withstand the weight of her shattered illusions a moment longer.

"You don't have to do anything you don't want to do," Mark reminded her. "Vanessa, you don't have to go back."

"Captain, you are not helping matters here," Oscar stated. "Your presence is no longer needed."

"Don't even think about it," Mark warned the smaller man, who looked as if he was about to order his security men to deal with Mark. They all halted in their tracks, unaccustomed to hearing a U.S. Marine officer bark an order. The voice was universally effective at making men obey.

Returning his attention to her, he said, "Vanessa, listen to me—"

"Why should I listen to you?" she interrupted him.

Clearly his officer voice didn't work at making this princess obey him. "Why should I listen to a single thing you have to say?"

"I'm sorry I had to deceive you—"

She interrupted him again. "You *had* to deceive me? And why was that? Was someone holding a loaded gun to your head, Captain?"

"I was following orders."

"Ah, yes. Just a loyal Marine. Following orders. Nothing personal." With every word another small part of her died. She should have listened to him that very first day, when he'd warned her that her Cinderella glass slippers were going to get broken in the real world. He hadn't warned her that he'd also shatter her heart.

She yanked the slipper necklace from her neck, breaking the delicate chain and leaving a red mark on her skin. She dropped the necklace onto the coffee table with the bitter knowledge that unlike Cinderella, there was no fairy-tale happy ending in sight for her.

"I had to do it," Mark was saying. "I couldn't disobey my orders."

"Weren't you the one who said 'I'm a Marine, I don't do anything against my will'?"

Oscar impatiently interrupted them. "Your Highness, we are wasting time."

"Put a sock in it," Mark warned Oscar. Facing Vanessa, he tried to defend his actions. "I didn't ask for this assignment."

Wrong thing to say. He saw that the moment the words left his mouth. He could feel the tension emanating from her. She was a land mine ready to detonate, and she did.

"I'm so sorry you were burdened with the assignment, Captain!'' Her green eyes flashed with fury. ''But look on the bright side. Your job is over now.''

''It wasn't just a job.'' His voice was clipped. ''*You* weren't just a job.''

''Right,'' she scoffed. ''I'll bet you say that to all the princesses you deceive.''

''Look, I know you're upset right now.''

''Upset doesn't even come close,'' she said, trying to keep the anguish at bay.

Later, she thought detachedly. Later she would allow herself to feel ashamed at the way she'd offered herself to him, the way she'd responded to his kisses. But not now. Not in front of him. Not in front of anyone.

''We've taken the liberty of packing your things, Your Highness,'' Oscar said. ''The private jet is waiting.''

''Let it wait,'' Mark growled, sending him a lethal look that had Oscar taking a step back. ''You're not taking her anywhere against her will.''

''Of course…we would never…'' Oscar sputtered.

''There is nothing of importance here that I need to take with me,'' Vanessa said in a painfully polite voice.

''What about those hopes and dreams you shared with me?'' Mark said.

''The ones you told my father about?'' she retorted. ''Do you mean those hopes and dreams? Did you include those in the reports you sent my father? I'd like to see them someday. I'm sure they'd be fascinating reading.'' There was a wealth of bitterness in her words.

His betrayal cut through her like a fiery sword being driven into her very soul. She'd loved him. She thought she'd found the one man who could love her for herself. She'd bared her soul to him, she'd told him things she hadn't revealed to anyone else. And now he had the nerve to talk about her hopes and dreams, after he'd just pulverized them all.

She'd *trusted* him. With her innermost thoughts, with her confessions, with her very heart.

And all the while, he'd gone to his laptop computer every night to relay it all back to her father, who'd betrayed her as well.

Her own father didn't appear capable of loving her. Why should she think that Mark could love her? Maybe it was her. Maybe there was some fatal flaw in her.

She stared at the royal coat of arms on the royal security guards' jackets with eyes too dry to cry. Misery clawed at her heart as a child's rhyme played in her head. All the king's horses and all the king's men…couldn't put one shattered princess back together again.

And shattered she certainly was, standing here with only one sandal. She tore it off and quickly slipped on her original walking shoes, which she'd carelessly left by the front door. She had to get out of here.

"You wanted to live a life that completed you instead of one that left you empty," Mark reminded her.

"Don't you dare throw my words back at me," she said fiercely, her control strained to the limit.

"Her Highness lives a very full life," Oscar stated. "Her fiancé is eagerly waiting for her return."

"Fiancé?" Mark went very still.

"Sebastian de Koonan is one of our wealthiest citizens," Oscar bragged. "His family has been connected to the royal family for generations. He is a successful business tycoon and a man of sophistication and class. He will make a fine and worthy husband for our princess."

Why wasn't Vanessa saying anything, why wasn't

she denying it? Mark stared at her, willing her to look him in the eye. Instead, a gulf of silence separated them. He tried to bridge it. "You told me there weren't any besotted beaux in the picture."

"Sebastian is in Volzemburg."

She wasn't denying it. There *was* a fiancé. Rich. Suitable. All the things he wasn't. Fury consumed him. "So what, that means out of sight out of mind with you?"

"My private life is none of your business." His snort of disbelief made her want to hurt him just a tenth as much as he'd hurt her. "Did you really think a princess like me would want a Marine like you?"

His face was instantly wiped clean of all expression. She'd made a direct hit, but the knowledge gave her no pleasure. She had to leave—*now,* before she broke down entirely. As if sensing her distress, Oscar placed a velvet cloak over her shoulders and guided her toward the door. Tucking the ends of the cloak around her body with numb fingers, Vanessa tucked the raw edges of her emotions deep inside, where no one could see them, where no one could access them and use them to hurt her.

"Dumb me for feeling guilty about deceiving you, Princess." His voice was gritty. "You were the one deceiving me all along."

"We deceived each other," Vanessa said, staring at him with green eyes dark with pain before walking out with Oscar and the guards.

Leaving Mark alone in an empty apartment, staring down at the silver slipper she'd left behind.

Chapter Ten

"**Y**our performance in this matter is a serious disappointment to me, Captain."

"I'm sorry, sir," Mark replied the next morning as he stood in his C.O.'s office at the Marine Combat Center in Quantico, Virginia. He'd taken the first flight out of New York and arrived here at 0900 hours. He hadn't gotten any sleep at all last night after Vanessa had left. That didn't matter. Marines didn't need sleep. They didn't need love either. Not from a princess engaged to another man.

Mark yanked his thoughts back to his current surroundings. The office was filled with standard government-issued desk, office chairs, bookcases and filing cabinets. In one corner stood the American flag, while prominently displayed in the opposite corner was the Marine Corps flag. Lined up around the wall in immaculate precision were framed photographs of Marine greats like Chesty Puller.

Mark's C.O., Lieutenant Colonel Charles Wilkes, had

the square-jawed face and military haircut of Chesty. He also possessed his own brand of steely-eyed stares that could be as piercing as a saber.

Lieutenant Colonel Wilkes used that stare on Mark as he stated, "Sorry doesn't cut it in the Marine Corps, Captain."

No excuses, no exceptions. The philosophy of every Marine. Mark nodded. "Understood, sir."

"You should know that."

"Yes, sir." There was a lot Mark should have known. Like the fact that Vanessa was engaged to some tycoon back in Volzemburg. Why hadn't that tidbit shown up on the files he'd been given?

"I understand that the king's press officer and the royal security guards walked in on you and the princess in a…compromising situation."

"Actually, sir, for the record, we walked in on them." Mark's voice was as crisp as the Marine uniform he wore. "They were waiting for us in the apartment." Ready to ambush us. Mark didn't say that, he just thought it. The door had been locked when he and Vanessa had arrived, which meant the royal security guards must have picked the lock and then relocked it once they were inside.

"And what if they'd been hostiles instead of the king's men? What would have happened to the princess then, Captain Wilder?"

"She would have been in danger, sir." Regret shot through Mark. Regret for so many things, he didn't even know where to start. Regret that he'd been given this assignment in the first place, regret that he'd let his emotions get out of hand, regret that he'd put her safety at risk, regret that he'd been taken in by her beauty. "That was a major error in judgment on my part, sir."

"Yes, it was. The question is what are we going to do about it?"

"Learn from it, sir." Oh, he'd learned all right. Learned it didn't pay to trust a sexy princess. All that time he'd been upset about having to deceive her, and she'd been lying to him the entire time.

"We expected better of you, Captain."

Letting down his fellow Marines was a black mark indeed against any Marine. The corps could only flourish if its values were respected—honor, courage, commitment.

Mark had let the Marine Corps down, and in doing so, had also let his own family down. His father was a Marine, as were his grandfather and great-grandfather. He'd blemished their honor by failing to accomplish this mission to the standards of their beloved corps. His humiliation ran deep. "I'm aware of that, sir, and I deeply regret the mistakes I made."

His C.O. closed the file on his desk. "At least the princess has finally returned to Volzemburg. She's not a Marine Corps problem any longer, she's her father's problem now."

Mark wished he could dismiss her as easily as his C.O. just had. And as a tough Marine he should have been able to boot her out of his thoughts. But he couldn't.

Which made him a real dope. She'd played him like a pro, wearing her flirty capri pants and smiling at him, kissing him and tempting him when all the while she was engaged to some millionaire back home. What an idiot he'd been.

He never should have trusted her. And to think she'd made him question his loyalty to the Marine Corps.

Made him think about the possibility of opening a security firm of his own.

She couldn't have done that if you didn't have questions of your own to begin with, his inner voice countered. He'd reached a crossroads in his career and maybe she was just the catalyst that got him thinking about things. Maybe it was time he made his own way, rather than following Marine Corps tradition, as fine as that tradition was.

Mark felt as if he'd put his head in a cement mixer, with his thoughts tumbling round and round.

"I'm aware that this mission was out of the ordinary, Captain. You've got an excellent record with the corps, and while we are disappointed that things turned out as they did, you did accomplish the main goal of maintaining the princess's security and of reporting her activities to King Leopold. I saw the e-mailed reports you sent in, Captain. While it is extremely unfortunate that you and the princess were caught in the aforementioned compromising situation, the king should have been more forthcoming in his explanation of the princess's engagement. But regardless of that, it was totally inappropriate for you to engage in any sort of romantic or sexual activity."

"No sexual activity occurred, sir," Mark curtly stated.

"I'm relieved to hear that, Captain." The lieutenant colonel tossed the file in his out bin. "As I said, this was an extremely unusual mission, and I for one am relieved that it's over with. This sort of thing is better left to the people at the State Department. It's not something the Marine Corps should be bothered with."

"Agreed, sir."

"As I said, you've got an outstanding record, Captain."

"Thank you, sir."

"I believe you were scheduled to take some liberty time before you were given this assignment. Is that right, Captain?"

"Affirmative, sir."

"Then take said leave. Mother's Day is coming up, Captain. Having met your mother, I'm sure she'd appreciate a visit from you."

"Affirmative, sir."

"Oh, I almost forgot. This came for you."

He handed Mark an envelope with a royal seal on it. "That will be all, Captain."

"Yes, sir." Mark saluted before pivoting and leaving his C.O.'s office behind. His internal misgivings remained with him, however, and showed no signs of abating as he opened the envelope. Inside was a check and a single sheet of richly embossed stationery from Her Highness Princess Vanessa Alexandria Maria Teresa Von Volzemburg.

For Your Expenses, she'd written and then itemized every single thing he'd gotten for her—every cab ride, the pizza, the meal at the fast-food restaurant, the ferry ride, everything, no matter how small.

He angrily ripped the check into tiny pieces and dropped it in a nearby trash can. He didn't need her money. He didn't need *her.*

"Why do you always have to make things so difficult for His Majesty?"

Vanessa had been hearing that same question the entire flight home yesterday from Oscar and from Hans, the head of security. She didn't need to be hearing it from her sister, Anna.

Her younger sister always referred to their father as His Majesty when she was trying to make a point. She was clearly trying to make a point now.

"Give me a break, would you please?" Vanessa said before slumping into the only comfortable chair in the Blue Drawing Room.

Normally this was one of her favorite rooms in the St. Kristoff palace. It had a sunny southern exposure and was furnished in a playful rococo style. But today the richly decorated ceilings felt as if they were pressing down on her.

Her sister compounded that feeling. Only eighteen months younger than Vanessa, Anna was petite and dainty like their mother. She shared the same coloring as Vanessa, green eyes and blond hair. But her hair was longer, and like Anna herself, more obedient. It always fell perfectly into place.

Anna had an appetite for royal duties. She excelled at riding and entertaining. She had a head for governing and could be as Machiavellian as their father about the politics of interacting with Volzemburg's elected assembly.

"I don't know how you could have been so rude to Sebastian," Anna was saying as she automatically straightened a pair of Meissen figurines so that they were exactly six inches apart on the gilt-wood table. "Standing him up to stay in New York City that way." She made a tsking noise of disapproval. "Your latest escapade has upset our father terribly."

"That makes us even then because his behavior has upset me terribly as well."

Anna frowned at her. "You've spent too much time in America. You're starting to sound..."

"Sound what?" Vanessa challenged her. "Like a real person?"

"Like a common person."

"If you think being heir to the throne is such a great job then maybe you should take it. Then you could be engaged to Sebastian."

Anna blinked away sudden tears. "That's not amusing."

Her sister's emotional reaction took her by surprise. Anna was the perfect daughter. Which meant she always had things under complete control.

"Come on, Anna, you know it's true. You'd make a much better future queen than I would. You're much more obedient, and you have a talent for governing that I totally lack. I just want everyone to get along, but you make sure they do lest they face your wrath. I can't do wrath very well."

Anna's momentary emotional display was replaced with a chilly glare.

"See," Vanessa said with a slight smile. "That's the perfect look of wrath. You're much better at it than I am."

"I may look like our mother, but you got her American independence." Anna did not make it sound like a compliment.

"Our mother was the perfect queen. I wish I could do half as well as she did, but that doesn't seem to be happening." Vanessa straightened her shoulders. She might be battered and badly bruised by Mark's betrayal, but she wasn't completely broken. She refused to be.

On the plane trip home she'd caught herself falling into a dull acceptance as she sat there in a maze of pain.

But when she'd reached the palace, she knew she couldn't allow herself to be talked into once again trying to please those she loved. Let them try to please her for a change!

"I'm telling you, Anna, I am *not* marrying Sebastian," Vanessa firmly declared. "No matter what Father says. The days when a king can order his daughter to marry someone are over. Mother would never have approved of this. She and Father married because they fell in love. That's what I want."

"Were you in love with the American Marine?"

Vanessa's heart cracked a little more each time she thought of Mark. Just when she thought she couldn't hurt any more than she already did, the pain welled deep within her again. "I don't want to talk about him."

Anna sat down in the chair beside her, leaning close to say, "Is it true that Oscar caught you kissing the Marine?"

Vanessa winced. "Why this sudden curiosity in my love life?"

"As I said, I don't think it's proper for you to treat Sebastian the way you have."

Thoroughly aggravated by now, she said, "If you like him so much, you marry him."

"I wish I could!" Anna suddenly burst out, leaping to her feet with tears running down her face. "But he never notices me!"

Vanessa was stunned. Anna loved Sebastian? "Oh, Anna, I'm so sorry. I had no idea." The next thing she knew, Vanessa was crying, too. Crying for her sister, crying for herself, crying for lost dreams that Mark was the man for her, that he loved her the way she loved him. How could she have been so foolish?

Love clearly affected a woman's vision, especially when that woman was a princess.

"Excuse me, Your Highnesses." Celeste stepped into the drawing room before freezing. "I'm so sorry. I didn't mean to interrupt."

Anna looked mortified at having been caught crying by the lady-in-waiting. Vanessa was beyond caring about appearances. "It's all right, Celeste. My sister and I were just having a good cry about men."

A big tear slid down Celeste's cheek as she sniffed, "They are all rotten! How could Abraham have deceived me like that? I thought he liked me, but he was involved in Captain Wilder's deception. That's the only reason he kept stopping by to see me at the hotel in New York."

Betrayal. Vanessa knew all about it. Being struck down by the one person you trusted above all others, the one man who'd made her feel safe and loved. But it had all been a sham. He'd only been following orders, orders placed by her father.

She handed a box of facial tissues to her sister and then to Celeste before taking one for herself.

Yes, men were indeed rotten. And being betrayed by the man you loved was even more rotten.

Mark's parents were waiting for him at the Phoenix Airport. After retiring from the Marine Corps, his dad and mom had moved to Arizona where his dad worked on improving his golf game and his mom was taking classes at the local community college to finally complete her college degree.

"You didn't have to come meet me," Mark said as they waited for him at the gate. "I could have rented a car."

His mom hugged him while his dad gave him one of those powerful backslaps he was famous for. "So you survived baby-sitting that princess, huh?" his dad said in his booming gravelly voice.

"Now, Bill," his mother scolded, "the boy just got off the plane. Give him a few minutes before you bombard him with questions."

"Me? You're the one who was worrying about some wealthy princess turning your son's head with her ritzy European ways."

"Oh, stop." She playfully slapped her husband's arm. "I was not worrying. We met Vanessa at Joe's wedding, and she seemed very nice."

Just the sound of her name made Mark flinch. He refused to think about her anymore. He'd already spent hours staring into that stupid snow globe she'd left behind, wondering what could have been, wondering what she was doing and if she was doing it with Sebastian.

After she'd left, he'd almost ended up throwing the snow globe against the wall and smashing it to bits. Instead, he had it tucked in his duffel bag along with the silver-slipper necklace and the two pieces of clothing the guards hadn't packed—those damn capri pants and the I Love NY T-shirt she'd slept in. It still smelled of carnations, of her. How sick was he? He told himself he was going to mail everything off to Prudence and have her forward it on. He told himself he could donate the stuff to Goodwill and let someone get some use out of it.

He told himself a lot of stuff, but the bottom line was that he had to stop thinking about her or he'd go crazy. Instead, he focused his attention on his parents. Despite the many moves, despite his father's dedication to the

Marine Corps, their relationship had always been bed-rock firm.

To his mom, her sons would always be ''the boys.''

To his dad, they'd always be…Marines.

But what happened if Mark decided he didn't want to continue being a Marine?

Emotion gripped Mark, making his stomach burn. He was an officer, for God's sake, trained to make split-second decisions as well as long-term plans. Yet here he was, mired in indecision and filled with frustration about his own future.

The truth was that he'd been wanting to punch some-one or something ever since the royal minions had swept Vanessa away from him. An array of intense emotions were there, right beneath the surface, ready to boil over if he didn't keep a tight lid on them.

His dad didn't notice anything amiss, but Mark could tell by the anxious looks his mom was giving him that she sensed something was up.

As always, he tried to batten down his emotional hatches, and keep going as if nothing was wrong. You do your job and you keep going. It was that simple. No excuses, no exceptions.

That evening Mark let off steam by going into the basement and taking his frustrations out on his dad's punching bag. He was furious with Vanessa for playing him for a fool. *Wham.* A fierce right hook to the bag. He was furious with himself for falling for her act. *Wham, wham.* How could he have been so stupid? *Wham, wham, wham.* He heard her words, playing like a tape in his head—Did you really think a princess like me would want a Marine like you? And her prissy note: For Your Expenses…

Whamwhamwhamwhamwham...

"Whoa there, son," his dad said from the basement steps. "You keep taking out your aggression on that bag and you're going to knock it into the next block."

Sweat poured down Mark's face as he stood there panting.

"You want to calm down a minute and tell me what's bothering you?"

Mark lifted his head and faced his father. Exhaustion had taken hold, allowing the words to just tumble out. "You never told me what you thought about my becoming an officer. Why is that?"

His dad blinked. "Where in the Sam Hill did that come from?"

Mark shrugged, not wanting him to see how much he cared. "The family has a long tradition in the Marine Corps, but as enlisted men. Not as officers."

"Enlisted men are the backbone of the Marine Corps."

The avid pride in his father's voice stung. Grimly, Mark demanded, "Which makes me what? Excess baggage? A staff weenie?"

"You are and always will be a United States Marine." The words were delivered in the booming voice of a drill sergeant.

Mark responded by shaking his head. "I'm not so sure about that."

His father faltered slightly. "What do you mean?"

"I might want something more."

"More than the Marine Corps?" Now his father looked horrified. "Where is all this crazy talk coming from? Did that princess mess up your brain? Is she trying to talk you into quitting the Marine Corps and going back to be her consort or something?"

"She hates me," Mark stated flatly.

"Then she's plain stupid, princess or no. If she can't see what a fine man you are, then I say good riddance to her."

"You still haven't answered my question." Now that he'd gone this far, Mark wasn't backing down. He'd wondered and stewed about this for years. It was time to finally get things out into the open. "When I first told you I wanted to become an officer, you got this look on your face. It wasn't the look of a proud father."

His dad paused before squaring his shoulders and looking Mark directly in the eye as he admitted, "It was probably the look of a father afraid that his son thought being an enlisted man wasn't good enough, that his father wasn't good enough."

Mark was stunned by his words. "How could you ever think that? I just wanted you to be proud of me. I wanted to be the best I could be."

"Son, I'm always proud of you," his father declared gruffly, before slapping him on the back so hard Mark winced and then smiled. "Even when you go and do something stupid like fall for a princess."

"I didn't, I haven't..." Mark sputtered.

His father simply nodded understandingly.

Mark swore softly and succinctly before sinking into his dad's ratty recliner that his mom had banished to the basement.

Again his father nodded understandingly and said, "I think it's time for a beer, don't you?"

"Forget the beer," Mark said wearily. "Get out the good stuff. Get out the scotch."

"I can't believe you were stupid enough to fall in love with a U.S. Marine," Anna said to Vanessa. She'd been acting snippy ever since she'd let down her hair and cried yesterday.

Vanessa had escaped to their private royal apartments, but Anna had simply followed her. They were both trying to avoid Sebastian. Vanessa was keeping herself busy by going through storage boxes of personal items, as if searching for herself in the mementos of her life.

This bedroom was known as the Queen Adrianna Bedroom, named after one of Volzemburg's most famous queens who ruled during the time of Queen Victoria. She may have been a wonderful queen, but her taste in furnishings was lavish and overbearing. The walls were covered in red velvet and all the furniture was covered with rich gold decorations. Vanessa had had to move in here after her mother died. Tradition dictated that on her sixteenth birthday, the heir to the throne would reside in this room.

It had always given her nightmares.

"As the royal family we're supposed to set the standard," Anna continued.

"Mais absolument." The announcement came from the doorway. Countess Desiree Dupres-Konig-Bernini stood in the threshold in all her sophisticated and colorful glory. Their godmother.

Her short dark hair was cut in the latest style to show off her high cheekbones and brilliant green eyes. She was their father's first cousin, and the only person on the planet who was bossier than he was. She was also one of the few people on the planet who could intimidate him. She didn't show up often at the palace—Vanessa hadn't seen her since her own twenty-first birthday party and before that at her mother's funeral.

"Come, *leiblings*, your godmother has arrived. Let the fun begin!"

Vanessa and Anna just looked at her.

"Why the long faces, *mignonnes?* Come, tell your favorite godmother all about it. What has that wickedly stubborn father of yours done now?"

"He wants me to marry Sebastian, whom I don't love at all," Vanessa replied.

"Vanessa is in love with a Marine," Anna said.

"Anna is in love with Sebastian," Vanessa replied in kind.

"Ah." Desiree nodded. "So this is all about love. *Naturellement*, love is something about which I know a great deal."

Desiree had been married three times, her current husband was an Italian count, and they lived in a palazzo on the Grand Canal in Venice. Desiree spoke fluent German, French, Italian and English and enjoyed mixing them all up.

"What are you doing here?" Vanessa asked.

"I came for the masquerade ball to celebrate your father's sixtieth birthday," Desiree replied, floating closer to elegantly drape herself into a chaise lounge. No one could lounge the way Desiree did. She was wearing a gorgeous shantung pantsuit in a mint green. "But enough about me, I want to hear about your Marine, Vanessa."

A blessed numbness had set in since her crying jag of yesterday, but now the pain returned. She tried to shrug it off. "He's just someone Father hired to spy on me while I was playing hooky in New York City."

"Hooky," Desiree repeated with a laugh. "What quaint sayings Americans have. And the talk about setting standards?"

"I want to do more than set the standards for things like this year's shoe fashion or flower arrangement," Vanessa said, her voice vehement. "I want to set the standards for the treatment of innocent children who can't take care of themselves!"

Then do it, a voice within Vanessa said. *Just do it.*

"You should be focusing on your wedding," Anna said.

"I told you, there isn't going to be a wedding," Vanessa declared. "At least not one between me and Sebastian. Why don't you go after him? The masquerade ball is coming up, that would be the perfect opportunity for you to make him see you with new eyes. I'm sure Desiree can help."

"*Mais oui,* I'm sure I can," the older woman instantly agreed. "Help you *both.* I have brought the most delicious costumes for the two of you. No one makes costumes like the Italians. And I found this for you, Vanessa. It's something I have been meaning to give you. Your mother wanted you to have it on your twenty-first birthday, she entrusted it to me as your godmother, but I was going through that messy divorce at the time, and my things were all in storage. Anyway, I have brought it to you now."

She handed over a book of poetry. Vanessa opened the leather-bound volume to find her mother's handwriting.

To Thyne Own Self Be True.
Happy Twenty-first Birthday, my darling Vanessa.

Vanessa blinked back the tears as she traced her mother's writing with her fingertips. In that instant she knew what she had to do.

When her sister went upstairs with their godmother to try on the costume she'd brought, Vanessa took the opportunity to make some phone calls. By the end of the afternoon, she'd fulfilled a lifelong dream.

She'd started her own foundation, Safe Haven for Children. In the end, it wasn't that hard to do. Perhaps the hardest things were actually the easiest ones when everything was said and done. It was all a matter of overcoming her need to please others and replacing it with the need to be true to herself and the need to help others.

Those words from her mother had seemed fate's way of reminding her of that fact.

"This is your sister-in-law calling, and I'm going to kill you."

"Why, hello to you, too, Prudence," Mark drawled into the phone, pressing a hand to his throbbing forehead before reaching for the bottle of aspirin his mom kept next to the stove in the kitchen. He and his dad had made quite a dent in that bottle of scotch last night.

"Don't give me that Wilder charm."

"How did you know I was here?" he interrupted her.

"I was calling your mother, and she said you'd come to visit. How could you spy on Vanessa like that?"

"Vanessa told you," he said in resignation.

"Of course she told me. I'm the one who recommended you to Vanessa, the one who assured her you were trustworthy."

"You shouldn't have involved me in the first place. Once you did, I was just following orders."

Her growl told him that she wasn't cutting him any slack because of that. "What horse manure!"

"Her father bugged her phone at the Plaza. He heard

Vanessa plotting with you. He called the State Department, and they called the Marines, who called me. None of this was my idea. I was just following orders," he repeated.

"Horse manure," Prudence repeated. "At one time, my father ordered Joe not to see me. I'll tell you the same thing I told them both, the Marine Corps has no business butting in."

"This could have caused an international incident. Besides, that princess buddy of yours wasn't exactly honest herself."

"What are you talking about?" Prudence demanded in an offended voice.

"I'm talking about that fiancé of hers back in Volzemburg."

"You mean Sebastian?"

Mark's stomach rolled. "So you know about him, too."

"Vanessa is not engaged to Sebastian. Sure, her father wants her to marry him, but she's not going to do it."

"That's not what she told me."

"She doesn't love Sebastian. There's no way she'd marry him."

For the first time, a flicker of hope. "Then why didn't she say that when those royal guys were talking about her engagement?"

"Because she'd probably prefer you think she was a bored princess toying with you than know the truth, that she'd fallen in love with you."

"Did she tell you that?"

"She didn't have to. I know her. You broke her heart."

Anguish replaced the anger that had been eating him

up, as Mark realized how much his deception must have hurt Vanessa. "I...I regret that more than I can say." His ragged voice was rough with despair.

He didn't tell his sister-in-law about feeling torn between his duty to the Marine Corps and his newfound love for Vanessa. What was the point? It didn't change anything.

"So what was she to you?" Prudence demanded. "Just a another special op, another Marine Corps mission?"

"No!" he said harshly. "I loved her."

"Then—"

He cut her off. "It doesn't make any difference. There's nothing I can do. She hates me now. Besides, she's a princess. She has everything. What could I possibly offer her?"

"The most valuable thing of all," Prudence gently but firmly replied. "True love. It's something Vanessa has been searching for all her life, and you're the one man who can give that to her. If you're brave enough to do that. Are you brave enough, Mark? Are you brave enough to go after her?"

Chapter Eleven

"What do you mean?" King Leopold bellowed at Vanessa. They were in the King's Dining Room, with its emerald-green silk walls framed by exquisitely carved oak panels and a dozen ionic columns in malachite. All day yesterday Oscar had been telling her that the king was far too busy to speak to her, so she'd ambushed him at breakfast this morning. "What do you mean you've started your own foundation? That is not your place."

"Yes, it is, Father. I've been trying to tell you that for the past hour."

"And what of your marriage with Sebastian? Did you consult him before taking this rash action?"

"It is not a rash action and no, I did not consult with Sebastian because it does not concern him." She gazed at her favorite painting, a Constable of a serene English countryside, in order to keep her composure in light of her father's stubbornness. The painting had been one of her mother's favorites as well. *To Thyne Own Self Be True*.

"Not concern him? He is your fiancé."

Her eyes shot from the painting to her father. "No, he is not!"

"Is this about that Marine you were kissing in Central Park?"

"Wha...at?" His question stunned her.

"You heard me. Is this about that Marine?"

"How did you know I kissed him in Central Park? Did you have people spying on us?" Vanessa demanded.

She remembered Mark's maneuvers to ensure they wouldn't be followed from the park because he'd been suspicious that someone was watching them. Apparently he'd been right.

Her father didn't look in the least bit repentant. "Naturally I arranged to have my firstborn daughter, the heir to the throne, protected."

"And who is going to protect me from you, Father? Can you answer that question?"

"I am your father and your king. You don't need protecting from me."

"Yes, I do," she said sadly. "Because you are more king than father. You aren't caring for your daughter, you are protecting your own vision of the future at her expense. Can't you see that? Can't you see what you're doing to me?"

For the first time since her mother died, she let him see the pain he'd caused her with his disapproval and criticism, with his constant emotional detachment. Eventually his expression changed until he looked almost stricken. "I did it for you. If you are to rule, you must be tough."

"I am tough. In many ways. But not in the ways that matter to you as king. That's why I think it would be best that the crown pass to Anna instead of me."

"That is impossible."

"No, it's not. It's happened before. I checked with Desiree. And she told me that Queen Adrianna was actually the second-oldest child. The history books don't bring that up, but she showed me the family bible. The oldest child was Kristina."

"She went into a nunnery," her father retorted. "Is that what you are planning on doing?"

"She had a higher calling. So do I. I want to make a difference in those children's lives. And the restrictions placed on me as the future queen of Volzemburg prevent me from doing that. Anna is the one who should be queen. You know she'd do an exceptional job at it. And she'd be much more willing to marry Sebastian than I am. This is the best thing for both your daughters, Father. It also happens to be the best thing for the Crown of Volzemburg."

He looked at her as if finally realizing he couldn't change her mind—or her. "Have you spoken with Anna about this?"

"I wanted to speak to you first. I'm sorry to have disappointed you all these years." Her voice was choked with emotion. "I really did try hard to be the kind of daughter you wanted me to be."

His eyes held more than a hint of melancholy as he softly said, "You are so much like your mother."

Vanessa shook her head. "I wish I were, but I'm not."

"Oh, but you are." He reached out to touch her cheek. "You are just as fiercely independent as she was. When she was pregnant with you and there were complications, it didn't matter that we had excellent doctors here. She wanted to return home to America and she went. She was very headstrong, and once she got an idea into her head there was no changing her mind. Yes, you are very much like her.''

''Then how could she handle being queen?''

''Because she loved me. She did it for me. I thought perhaps if you could grow to love Sebastian, you would curb your independence because of your love. But instead you fell in love with an American Marine.''

''I'm not—''

He cut her off. ''I know you, Vanessa. You wouldn't be kissing a man in public the way you were if you didn't have strong feelings for him.''

''I'll get over him,'' she fiercely vowed. ''I'll be much too busy helping the children. We're hoping to launch a major fund-raiser soon.''

''Why not do that at the masquerade ball this weekend?''

His suggestion surprised her. ''But the ball is to celebrate your birthday.''

''What is that saying, something about killing two birds with one stone? We can do both. Celebrate my birthday and launch your new foundation.''

She eyed him suspiciously. ''Are you doing this because you think it will make me change my mind about the crown going to Anna?''

''No, I'm doing this because it is the right thing to do. I will go speak to Anna now. Despite what you think, I do love both my daughters. And I am sorry you felt you disappointed me. As you said, I was not viewing you as a father but as your king. No father could have wished for a more loving daughter, Vanessa.''

His quiet pronouncement brought her to tears as she

gripped his outstretched hand. "I love you, Father."
She hadn't said the words since she was a little girl.

If he turned her away now, her heart, already broken
by Mark, would never recover. His other hand trembled
as he placed it on her bent head. "I..." His voice
sounded rusty. "I love you, too."

"I have to be careful around the candles tonight, I
fear I may be flammable," Desiree declared with her
customary flair for drama. She was wearing a designer
dress with a puffed pink ostrich-feather skirt. She'd
scorned wearing a mask—"What, cover this gorgeous
face?" she'd said in outrage. On her left hand was the
flawless five-carat diamond ring the Italian count had
given her, and in her right hand was a silver magic
wand.

Vanessa thought she was carrying this godmother
thing a bit far, but then that was Desiree. She wasn't a
woman to do things in half measure. And neither was
Vanessa.

Tonight was the launch of her Safe Haven for Children Foundation. She'd been working nonstop the past
three days getting ready for it, so she was tired, but this
was a good kind of exhaustion, the kind that came with
knowing you were making a difference. Just from the
advance press coverage alone, they'd already gotten
enough donated funds to triple the nursery staff at the
orphanage in Romania she'd visited a few months ago.
Babies needed to be held and touched, or they didn't
develop emotional bonds and as a result had problems
that stayed with them long into adulthood. Increasing
the staff increased the ratio of adults to babies.

She'd also worked on setting up an exchange program with college students from Volzemburg volun-

teering several months of their time to simply hold the babies and rock them and talk to them. American hospitals had a similar program for premature infants who had to stay in the hospital.

It was wonderful finally being able to focus all her attention on the charity dearest to her heart.

There was no word from the *man* dearest to her heart. Not that she expected Mark to contact her. What was there left to say? He'd never told her he loved her, he'd just looked at her that way and kissed her that way.

No, she couldn't think about him tonight. She must not. This was the night for the foundation and for her father.

"Well, *mes enfants,* you look absolutely ravishing. Those dresses are simply divine."

Desiree had excellent taste. Both Vanessa and Anna were dressed like fairy-tale princesses in dresses that would have done Cinderella proud, with a tight bodice and waist flaring out to a full, long skirt with a slight train in the back. Anna's dress was in a lovely lavender shade while Vanessa's was white. Both wore diamond tiaras in their upswept hair. And both wore samples from the royal jewels—Anna had the sapphire set and Vanessa wore the diamond necklace their father had made for their mother. Their dresses' off-the-shoulder necklines displayed the jewelry to perfection as well as showing just a hint of cleavage.

Which worried Anna. "Are you sure it is proper to show so much..."

"Bosom?" Desiree said. "You want Sebastian to notice you, yes?"

"I have a certain standard to uphold now," Anna reminded her, referring to the announcement that would be made tonight.

"And you shall uphold it while upholding your bosom. Now come, *leiblings*." Desiree tapped them each on the shoulder with her silver wand. "It is time for us to make our grand entrance."

And grand it was, with the three women poised at the top of the palace's grand staircase leading directly to the royal ballroom. The floor on the stairway and the ballroom itself was laid in a beautiful pattern of different-colored marble. The mirrored walls reflected the gathered aristocratic crowd, all elegantly dressed in brightly colorful costumes with jewels flashing.

Liveried trumpeters, wearing the white and gold colors of state, heralded their arrival. "Their Highnesses, the Princess Vanessa Von Volzemburg and Princess Anna Von Volzemburg and the Countess Desiree Dupres-Konig-Bernini."

"Are you sure this is a good idea?" Abraham Rosenthal softly asked Mark as they gazed up at the St. Kristoff Castle.

Mark had studied the layout ahead of time. Inside the castle walls were the palace itself, residential buildings and a chapel. It stood on a hillside slightly above the quaint city of St. Kristoff, looking like a fairy-tale castle with its spires, towers and graceful lines.

The place was pretty intimidating. What could he offer a woman who lived in a place like this? Love, he reminded himself. True love, the kind that lasted a lifetime. He could only hope it would be enough.

"Crashing the king's party? You've thought this through?" Abraham inquired.

"I didn't ask you to come with me," Mark reminded him. "You were the one who insisted on tagging along."

"I figured you could use some backup. *Semper fi* and all that."

"Or did it have something to do with that quiet little lady-in-waiting?"

"She may be quiet, but she's feisty underneath."

"She may not be glad to see you," Mark warned him.

"Vanessa may not be glad to see you, either," Abraham retorted.

"That's a given. I'll just have to convince her otherwise."

"So you have a plan?"

"Plans haven't served me very well in dealing with Vanessa. I think this time I'll try something else," Mark said.

"And that would be?"

"Honesty. Now hand me that rope. We've got a castle wall to scale here."

Vanessa watched Sebastian dancing with Anna. There was no doubt that he was smitten. He'd stared at her as if seeing her for the first time. Vanessa was certain her sister and Sebastian would end up together.

Her sister was glowing. Taking on the position of inheriting her father's throne had brought her newfound confidence and happiness.

"Well, daughter, how does it feel to have given up a throne this evening?" King Leopold asked Vanessa as he joined her.

"It feels good. But I will miss the chocolate."

"The royal chocolatier asked me to tell you that you shall always have unlimited access to his wares. You are still a royal princess, you know."

"A working princess."

"You've always worked hard."

"Yes, but now my work is something that is fulfilling in a meaningful way. The evening has gone better than I could have imagined. We've already raised nearly half a million dollars to help the orphans."

"And the evening isn't over yet."

"That's right. We still have your birthday cake to cut in another hour or so. The royal baker has outdone himself this time, I'm told," she said with a teasing smile.

Her father appeared distracted, however. "I wonder where that godmother of yours has gotten to. I can see why her husband stayed behind in Venice. The woman is a menace."

"Now, young man, do you care to tell me what you are doing up here?"

Mark stopped short. He and Abraham had climbed over the battlements in the rear of the castle and entered through a tower door. The palace security needed beefing up, he'd have to speak to Vanessa about that. First he had to deal with this woman wearing the wild ostrich dress.

"What are *you* doing up here, ma'am?" Mark countered, stalling for time.

"I needed a cigarette." She blew tobacco smoke at him. "The king doesn't approve. I'm not sure the king would approve of you, either. You are Vanessa's Marine, aren't you?"

Mark wasn't about to admit to anything that might get him tossed out. Not when he was this close. "We're guests who lost our way."

"Wearing camouflage paint on your face?"

He shrugged. "It's a masquerade ball, right?"

"Yes. But one normally doesn't wear camouflage

paint with a Prince Charming costume. What look were you aiming for? Warrior prince?"

"I'm no prince," Mark muttered. He'd planned on wiping off the greasepaint as soon as they'd gotten inside, but then this woman brandishing a cigarette in one hand and a silver wand in the other had suddenly shown up.

Things were simply not going his way.

But he was not about to give up. He was a Marine...dressed like Prince Charming, right down to the stupid tights. Surely his costume alone proved he loved Vanessa. He certainly wouldn't look this ridiculous for anyone else.

He should have worn his dress blues uniform. It was in the rental car parked in the woods behind the castle. Then he wouldn't feel like such an idiot.

"I had Hans, the head of security, show me your picture," the woman informed him. "Those blues eyes of yours are quite distinctive, Captain Wilder. And your friend here must be the good Dr. Rosenthal. I'm actually quite delighted to make both your acquaintances."

Mark raised an eyebrow. "You are?"

"Certainly. I'm Vanessa's godmother, Desiree, and I must say it certainly took you long enough to get here."

"I came as fast as I could, ma'am."

"Yes, well, now that you're here we must get you out of those ridiculous costumes. Come along." Desiree marched down the corridor, fully expecting them to follow her. She was stunned when she reached the staircase to find no one behind her. The two Americans had simply disappeared.

Waiters served *bellinis* and a string quartet played Vivaldi as Vanessa moved from the Victoria Salon through the Yellow Salon and the Billiards Room back to the ballroom. She couldn't seem to settle in any one place. And then it happened. Across the crowded ballroom, reflected in the floor-to-ceiling mirrors, Vanessa caught sight of a man dressed in a United States Marines dress blues uniform.

Mark! Her heart leaped. He'd come.

Lifting her long skirt, she hurried across the ballroom, smiling and nodding at people who tried to speak to her, but not stopping until she reached him. He had his back to her.

"Mark?" She put her hand on his arm, and immediately realized her mistake. This man was shorter and heavier. And the uniform was just a costume, not the real thing. "I'm sorry," she whispered. "I thought you were someone else."

Disappointment shot through Vanessa. It was bone deep and intense, and it made her realize that even though she'd changed her life, something was still missing. Love.

The emptiness inside her was suddenly overwhelming.

Tears came to her eyes as she turned to hurry out of the ballroom before anyone could see her discomfort. As she rushed out the open French doors to the palace gardens, her right sequin-encrusted shoe fell off. The last time that had happened she'd been wearing inexpensive sandals and fleeing a brawl with Mark in New York.

That had been a pivotal moment for her, when he'd swept her up in his arms and made her feel so safe, so loved. It had been the moment when she'd realized she loved him with all her heart.

Perhaps she'd been too hard on him. He had only

been following orders. In fact, he'd said he'd agreed to come help her even before those orders had been placed. She hadn't believed him. Maybe she should have.

She wiped the tears from her cheeks and paused to sit on a concrete bench in the elaborate palace gardens. Flowers were geometrically arranged around her while clipped hedges lined carefully laid-out paths. She could smell the roses in the warm night air as she took a deep breath, trying to regain her composure.

"Lose something, Princess?"

That voice. Her heart stopped and then thundered. It couldn't be...

She turned.

It was! It was Mark. Dressed in his impressive Marine dress blues uniform with its high-necked navy-blue jacket with red piping and brass buttons. The real thing. Standing proud and confident, his stance military erect as he gazed at her with those gorgeous blue eyes of his.

"What are you doing here?" she whispered unsteadily.

"Looking for you. After scaling the castle walls and getting past your security people, who need improving by the way, I ran into your godmother who convinced me to change out of the ridiculous Prince Charming costume I was wearing. I'm not even going to go into what a challenge it was leaving the palace again to retrieve my uniform from the rental car, let alone to slip back inside again. Then I finally get to the ballroom and Abraham finds Celeste without any problem, but I can't find you. There are hundreds of people in there, all in costume and most of them wearing concealing masks. It was like New Orleans at Mardi Gras. I ended up asking a toga-wearing Caesar, a pair of giggling teenagers dressed as white mice and a rotund guy in a stupid pumpkin costume if they'd seen you. One of the white mice said you'd come this way. None of which is relevant.'' He finally paused long enough to draw in a brief breath of air. Vanessa had never heard him say so much.

"Forget I said any of that," he ordered.

She doubted this Marine of hers would ever get over his natural inclination to give orders. She looked forward to teaching him the finer art of other forms of persuasion.

"I need to start again," he was saying. "Lose something, Princess?"

Yes, her heart. Could he tell? Didn't he know how much she loved him?

Dropping to one knee before her, he gently slipped her shoe back on. Then he took something from his pocket. It was the silver-slipper necklace she'd torn from her neck in New York. "Granted, it's not a glass slipper and granted, I'm not Prince Charming," he said huskily, "but I really do love you, and I want to marry you."

She started shaking. This was too good to be true.

"I'm sorry I deceived you," he said, his voice now tight with emotion. "There are no words to express how sorry I am. I want you to forgive me. Do you think you can do that?"

Unable to speak past the lump in her throat, she could only nod.

"Trust is an essential part of leadership in the Marine Corps. Trust has to be earned. It's a product of familiarity and confidence. You trusted me and I abused that trust."

"Captain," she interrupted him with a teasing smile, "you're starting to sound like a Marine again."

"A Marine in love with a princess." He gazed at her with his heart in his eyes. It was all there laid bare for her to see. The remorse, the regrets, the pain, the nervousness, the love, the desire.

"I'm a princess in name only," she replied, her voice unsteady. He loved her! He'd just said it again. "I just gave my throne to my sister."

His expression could only be described as stunned. "Why?"

Did his reaction mean he wanted her because she was a princess? Surely not. "I did it because it's what I wanted, what she wanted and what's best."

Guilt consumed him. "Is this because of me? Did you lose your throne because of me?"

"I didn't lose it, I gave it back. And it's because of *me,* not anyone else," Vanessa assured him. "I was tired of pretending to be something I wasn't and never felt I could be. Tired of living a life that left me empty instead of completing me. I can't change my past, but I could change my future, so I did. I started that foundation I'd been dreaming of and it's already making a difference."

Looking in her eyes, Mark could see how she'd grown. She was no longer the willful princess he'd first met. She'd become a strong woman in charge of her own life, not ruled by her father's plans.

"Do you still want to marry me?" she asked him, looking into his eyes and seeing the admiration in his gaze. She knew, knew it was for her as a woman, not as a princess.

"Affirmative. I can't change my past, either. But I

want a future with you. I'm not planning on remaining in the Marine Corps indefinitely.''

''But you've always been a Marine.''

''And you've always been a princess.''

''Actually I still am a princess,'' she admitted ruefully, ''just not heir to the throne any longer.''

''Actually once you're a Marine, you are a Marine for the rest of your life,'' he admitted just as ruefully. ''Even if you're not actively serving in the Marine Corps.''

''What will you do instead?'' she asked.

''Wait for you to accept my proposal. Then tell you about my dream of opening a security firm—''

Vanessa's mind was already racing ahead. ''We could work together,'' she excitedly interrupted him. ''A Marine and a princess. You know security, and I know etiquette and diplomacy. You could call your company Sovereign Securities, for foreign diplomats living in America. I can run the Safe Haven for Children Foundation from anywhere.''

''Before you go naming our new business endeavor, don't you think you should accept my marriage proposal?'' Mark said with a grin. ''Or should I ask your father for your hand in marriage? You're the etiquette expert here. I should have brought a ring instead of a dumb slipper necklace. I'm not doing any of this right,'' he growled. ''I should have had a plan.''

She cupped his cheek to turn his face to hers. ''Don't call my necklace dumb, and I don't need a plan. I just need *you*.''

His blue eyes blazed at her. ''Does that mean…?

Vanessa nodded. ''Yes, I will marry you, Captain Mark Wilder. I hope you know what you're getting into because there's no backing out now.''

"A Marine never backs out, ma'am," Mark huskily assured her. "This Marine plans on loving you for the rest of my days…and nights."

Taking her in his arms, Mark trailed his fingertips along her cheek as his mouth slowly descended to hers. It was a kiss worth waiting a lifetime for, the kiss of the one man who could give her what she'd wanted most—true love.

Epilogue

Four months later

"Are you sure that's the necklace you want to wear with your wedding dress?" Desiree asked Vanessa.

Vanessa touched the silver-slipper necklace around her neck and smiled. "I'm absolutely positive."

"Nice palace you've got here," Prudence noted with a grin. "A little on the large side for me, though."

"Me, too," Vanessa agreed. "Mark found us this darling little house in Virginia. I can't wait to move in with him."

"I did warn you about these Wilder men. They can be irresistible."

"I still think you were plotting to make us sisters-in-law."

"I was hoping you and Mark would hit it off at my

wedding, but when the two of you totally ignored one another I decided you were both hopeless.''

''She is totally hopeless,'' Anna announced from the corner, where she was fastening pearls around her neck. ''That's why I'm the heir to the throne now.''

Vanessa, Prudence and Desiree responded by tossing the small silk brocade pillows adorning the couch at her.

''Is that any way to treat your future queen?'' Anna demanded with feigned outrage.

''You better behave,'' Vanessa warned her. ''Your wedding to Sebastian is coming next summer.''

''I know.'' Anna's expression became dreamy. ''I can't wait.''

''Speaking of waiting, I believe we've kept that captain of yours waiting long enough, Vanessa.'' Desiree checked her appearance once more in the mirror. She, Prudence and Anna all wore bridesmaids dresses the rich color of a cognac diamond. The V-waistline and simple but elegant lines were reminiscent of medieval times.

Vanessa's satin-and-lace white wedding gown incorporated the same delicate one-hundred-fifty-year-old Belgian lace used in her mother's wedding gown. The dress embodied everything she wanted to express today—where she'd come from, who she was, who she wanted to be. The simple lace-edged bodice with three-quarter sleeves was appropriate for the autumn wedding. The dropped waistline matched that of her attendants. The real magic of the dress was in how it fit her and how it made her feel.

As Prudence straightened the five-foot train, Vanessa gazed down at her engagement ring. She and Mark had shopped for it together. She'd gone with a sleek modern design, princess-cut diamonds channel-set in platinum. The wedding rings were simple platinum bands.

"Ready?" Prudence asked.

Vanessa nodded as her father joined her at the back of the royal chapel. He was wearing full regal attire and looked very handsome in his uniform, complete with the royal sash and medals. "You look lovely," he said. "Your mother would have been so proud of you. As am I." He held out his arm to her.

Blinking back tears, Vanessa took it.

As liveried trumpeters announced their imminent arrival inside the royal chapel, Prudence said, "I thought this was going to be a small ceremony."

"It is," the king replied. "We only have a hundred guests. Anna's wedding shall be in the cathedral with five hundred attending."

"Better you than me," Vanessa told Anna with a grin.

"I can't concentrate with all this chattering," Desiree protested. "As it is, all these gilded angels flying about on the ceilings and walls in here are giving me a headache. I need a cigarette."

"Don't you dare move," Anna ordered.

The doors opened and the wedding procession began as the St. Kristoff Children's Choir sang a hymn in Latin. Vanessa's eyes remained fixed on Mark waiting for her at the end of the aisle. Mark had teasingly asked her if she planned on wearing that Yankees baseball cap he'd given her. While she didn't go that far, she'd broken with tradition by wearing her chapel-length veil away from her face instead of covering it. She said it was because she wanted to see where she was going, that she didn't want to trip over her own big feet and suffer any more shoe mishaps.

But the truth was that she wanted to have a clear view of Mark. He looked every bit as strong and sexy as he had when he'd proposed to her. Once again he was wearing his Marine dress blues uniform, as was his brother and best man Joe. Mark's oldest brother, Justice, was on a mission and couldn't get away. His youngest brother, Sam, sat in the front row with his parents.

The rest of the groom's side of the chapel was filled with numerous Marines, flown over on a plane her father had chartered.

Vanessa's side held an eclectic blend of friends and family, some royal, many not. The entire board from the Safe Haven for Children Foundation was in attendance. The royal chocolatier was still putting finishing touches on their wedding cake but promised her he'd peek in on the ceremony as well. And her former lady-in-waiting, now personal assistant, Celeste, was there with her new husband, Dr. Abraham Rosenthal.

And then Mark's hand was on hers as he tucked her by his side. Sunlight streamed through the stained glass windows, bathing them in gloriously colored light as they stood before the rococo altar with its soaring columns, scrolls and angels.

When Vanessa had been a little girl, she used to come to the chapel on weekdays when no one was here, and she'd lie on the marble floor and gaze up at the angels and wonder what made them smile.

Now she knew. Love made them smile. Love made

her smile. It even made her U.S Marine captain smile.

"Do you, Princess Vanessa Alexandria Maria Teresa Von Volzemburg, take Captain Mark Anthony Wilder to be your lawfully wedded husband..."

"Mark Anthony?" she whispered to her about-to-be husband.

"This is no time to get cute," he warned her.

"No," she agreed, knowing the royal chaplain was hard of hearing due to old age and couldn't hear them if they didn't shout. "That's for later, in the bedroom."

"You've got that right," he said, intertwining his fingers with hers.

Realizing the chaplain was looking at her expectantly, Vanessa loudly said, "I do."

"And do you, Captain Mark Anthony Wilder, take Princess Vanessa Alexandria..."

"Did you pack that silky nightgown you showed me?" Mark whispered to her.

"Along with my beloved baseball cap."

"Should make for an interesting combination."

"I wouldn't want to clash. Maybe I should just wear the baseball cap and nothing else?" she murmured seductively. "Do you like that idea?"

The chaplain cleared his throat.

"I do! I absolutely do!" Mark declared loudly enough that everyone in the back row heard him clearly. They later commented on how forceful and certain a Marine officer's voice could sound.

They also commented on how forcefully he kissed his new bride as he took her into his arms the instant the chaplain pronounced them man and wife.

Vanessa only knew that her home was in this man's arms and that there was nowhere else she'd rather be.

* * * * *

Watch for Cathie Linz's
next Silhouette Romance,

A PRINCE AT LAST,

part of the
ROYALLY WED:
THE MISSING HEIRS *continuity.*
Cathie returns to her
MEN OF HONOR
miniseries with Justice Wilder's
story in 2002.

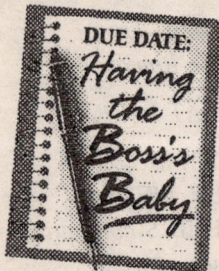

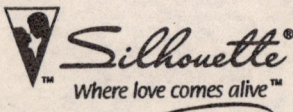

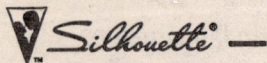

Silhouette

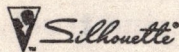

INTIMATE MOMENTS™
is proud to present

Romancing the Crown

*With the help of their powerful allies,
the royal family of Montebello is determined
to find their missing heir. But the search for the
beloved prince is not without danger—or passion!*

**This exciting twelve-book series begins in January and
continues throughout the year with these fabulous titles:**

Available at your favorite retail outlet.

Silhouette®
Where love comes alive™

Visit Silhouette at www.eHarlequin.com

SIMRC

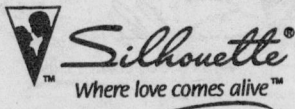